REDEMPTION 3
DEATH AT DOWNER'S GROVE
THE MIKE PARSONS TRILOGY

MALCOLM
TANNER

Publishing Coordinator – Sharon Kizziah-Holmes
Cover Design – Jaycee DeLorenzo

Paperback-Press
an imprint of A & S Publishing
A & S Holmes, Inc.

ISBN -13: 978-1-951772-13-0

DEDICATION

I dedicate this book to my parents, Charles and Barbara. The older I get, the more I go back and reminisce about the wonderful childhood I had and how they did all they could to support me. My love for them is endless.

ACKNOWLEDGMENTS

Thanks to Gail Mewes for help in the production of this work.

Thanks to Linda Knight, my editor. Linda worked tirelessly to make sure that I wrote exactly what I was trying to say. Her hours of dedication and purpose are greatly appreciated

Thanks to all the events in my life that changed both for good and bad that helped me and inspired me to write. All events in the book are purely fictional.

Thanks to Sharon Kizziah-Holmes, at Paperback Press, for the great interior design and formatting of this edition.

Thanks to Jaycee DeLorenzo, at Sweet-n-Spicy Design, for the beautifully done cover for this edition.

PROLOGUE

Joanna Presley and I landed back in Milwaukee. We had been through something together that I never thought would happen. Both of us knew the danger that still existed as we struggled to talk about what had happened.

We walked to get our cab and we were going to go back to my place. There was so much to take care of logistically, as so much had changed for us. Our world may never be what it was, but wherever it may take us, I was hoping that it would not change our bond, change our lives as a couple, as a pair, and as soul mates. Each step we were about to take was to be taken carefully, thoughtfully, and with each other's feelings in mind. I truly did not know whether or not we would make it. The danger alone could drive any woman away, but Joanna Presley was not just any woman. She came into my life when I needed someone the most. I was grateful for that. I wondered to myself if, after these kinds of events of kidnapping, violence, and danger that seemed to never end, would she just walk away? I needed her, and I think she knew that. Even so, my mind could see her walking out of my door at any time and never returning. I wouldn't blame her if she did just that. My heart, though, was hoping for the best.

We walked into my home and closed the door behind us. There was so much to say and so much to discuss. We had to find out where we were now, find our voices for each other again. But, right this minute, we turned to each other, looking straight into each other's eyes. I could feel her and she could feel me. The short distance between us was magnetic. That space was drawing us to each other. We embraced and I held her close. I could feel her fear along with her warmth and her caution. I could feel it all. We stood there a very long time saying nothing. It was like a cliff-hanging experience, gripping the rocks hard, and trying to hang on. We had to hang on. We just had to...

CHAPTER 1

It was Monday morning, the day after we had returned. I woke up in my bed with Joanna in my arms. We had not made love, but just held on, talking very little. I had just needed to feel her near me and wanted to keep her from leaving.

I quietly got out of bed and went to make coffee. It was near 5:30 and still dark but spring was well in sight. The Wisconsin air was beginning to feel fresh and new when I stepped out on my porch as the coffee was brewing. Still a bit chilly, the prospects of warmer days and possibly fishing with my brother, James, was something I could look forward to.

The thought of going to my lake place brought back the memories of the encounter with Allison Branch, Jerry Linhart, Breanne Jackson, Katy O'Neal, Andy Marx and me. I felt the gun shots, the fear, the physical and emotional pain, and I had to ask myself, if indeed, I could ever go back there again. I kept staring out at the horizon, looking for the sun to show its powerful orange glow on this Monday morning. I was hoping it could reveal the answers to the questions I had in my mind.

Why hadn't she killed me? She had plenty of opportunities to end my life. Why not? Even though it was cold, I felt the sweat running down my spine, dripping down my nose, beading up on my forehead. I know she is coming back for me, don't I? Every day of my life, until she is dead, I will have thoughts like these. Questions exists without answers. Danger is still there until she's stiff and cold. But can I pull the trigger? Can I?

Just then a hand gently touched my back. It made me jump a bit. I turned and I saw Joanna smiling at me.

"Why don't you come back inside? It seems kind of chilly out here," she said.

"Sure, sure, I was trying to see some morning glow before the coffee got done. Spring is almost here, and the thought of getting to the lake house more often was suddenly on my mind. I hope we can go there together sometime. I think you will like it," I responded.

"I'd love to, but for right now, can we skip the coffee? I want you to come back to bed with me," she said in a sultry voice and reaching up to kiss my cheek.

"I'd love nothing more, I need to feel you close to me," I said kissing her forehead and then her lips.

We walked to the room and shut the door. We made love and fell asleep in each other's arms. My mind needing clearing and it needed to rest. To forget everything except Joanna Presley was all that I wanted to do right now. Fortunately, my mind did just that. It wouldn't last long...

▲

Allison Branch had a lot of healing to do. She was in a place where she would have time to do it. The hills and forests, where the cartel housed its large compound, was a heavily armed fortress. It would be hard for any police to penetrate without a small army to help them. She would be safe here for a while, as she would need extensive treatment to recover.

Her face had been badly burned and this would take time, more time than she wanted it to. Her medications had to be renewed to calm her and kept her under control. She had gone off the deep end not taking them and she needed them to recover mentally, too. Taking her meds would help.

It was early Monday morning, and she had not slept well. Allison was still in a lot of pain and had slept only a few hours at a time. Her inner voice began to speak:

The explosion had done its damage, but I will recover. I will win and I will still hunt them down again. They got away twice, but the third time would be a charm. They won't be that lucky again. I will make sure, right? I'm a winner and those people are disgusting losers. They will pay, oh yes, they will pay...

Allison drifted off to sleep once more. Sitting in the chair in the corner of the bedroom was her keeper, the one who had made it his own private job to watch over her. Jake laid his head on the back rest of the chair. He was tired and he needed rest. He began to think of his sister and how she had betrayed him and the cartel. The Boss is surely going to go after her. As he closed his eyes, he saw their mother, watching them in the street playing with the other children. He loved his sister and it brought a smile to his face. But his smile quickly turned into a tight-lipped grimace. *How could she, damn her, how could she? She was a traitor and she had to be dealt with. But she is my sister and we have gone through so much together. Why am I so conflicted? She did wrong by the cartel rules, but she's my sister. What will I tell Mama? I have to go see her and let her know what happened and that the only way Maria was coming back was in a box. Mama may never see her again. And about Andres, I won't let Mama know that I know. I have to go see her today, that is if the Boss will let me...*

CHAPTER 2

Carrianne Martinez was still under protection of US Marshalls. She was about to become the main cooperating witness in the hunt for Branch, Jake and the cartel. Overnight, she had thought so much about Jake, her mother and her family. At this moment, there was no turning back. She had made her choice and she just wasn't sure of all the consequences that lie ahead.

She felt a deep pang in her heart for her mother. She would certainly miss her and the thought of never seeing her again had made her cry often. She had spent many months at a time not seeing her mother, even though she had always made some time to go back and see her in Rio. She tried to erase the vision of her mother's face, but it kept coming back, especially when she closed her eyes.

She didn't know what today, next week, or next year had in store for her. But for the moment, her biggest concern was how to tell the story of her involvement with the cartel, where they were located, who was in charge, and how they could bring all of them, including Branch, to justice. When she thought of Branch, she became still and her thoughts went back to Branch's eyes that demanded your attention and the conversation they had by the pool in Santa Teresa during Allison's recovery from plastic surgery.

Branch confided in her and listened to Carrianne's questions. She had thought at the time that she could like Branch. Her time spent with her turned to chaos, and Carrianne watched Branch get noticeably more unhinged every day. She knew Branch was someone to fear. Of that, she had no doubt. Carrianne began to feel a coldness coming over her body as she thought of what Branch was capable of doing. She wondered if Jake had been taken in by her and the danger that he might face. Carrianne and Jake had been through so much together, but he had changed and Allison Branch was the one that had changed him.

Today would be hours and hours of questions, descriptions and answers for the US Marshalls and FBI investigators. This was going to be a long journey to freedom. The freedom that she had dreamed about was going to be within her reach but would not come without a price. She was willing to pay that price. She was about to enter a world that she was so unfamiliar with, the world of coming clean and being a citizen, a wife, and possibly a mother. Motherhood was something she had dreamed of often. She could escape the cartel and its inherent dangers and she could have a life of her own. But the dangers of the cartel were also still hanging over her head because she knew the Boss and he would come after her. She had no idea what Jake would do to help the Boss, and she wished that he had chosen, like her, to escape the cartel. Jake had turned from her brother to the enemy that she hoped she would never see again.

So many conflicts, yet Carrianne was ready for her long days ahead. Today, she was stepping into a new world and it was her only hope of staying alive. It would take some time, but today was day one for Carrianne and she was ready to learn to write a new name over and over until she slowly became someone else. The road was going to be long, but her journey was starting today. Her chosen path would not always be smooth...it never had been.

Joanna and I had one more week to gather ourselves before returning to work. We had just arrived home but by Monday mid-morning, we had received several calls from reporters wanting to do interviews, which we declined. Andy told us to stay silent about the facts in an on-going investigation, and we would trust his wisdom on that.

James had called early in the morning as he wanted to catch up with me about all that he had heard on the news. I told him that I could possibly do that later, but for now, I had to keep quiet about it. James understood that, but as my brother and closest confidant, he certainly wanted to do what he could to help. We discussed a fishing trip, possibly in mid-summer, to get away for a while and get back in touch. I told him that I would be anxious to go fishing and I would let him know when I would be able go. Then we could talk.

Joanna, brought her cup of coffee with her and we sat together on the couch. She set her cup down and was leaning her head on my shoulder. I could feel her soft breathing against me. She looked up at me and smiled. I set my cup down also and put my arm around her, pulling her close to me.

"Just where do we go from here?" I asked. "The media is wanting interviews, Andy will be getting back to us soon, and we still have to go back to work sometime. I know we need to discuss us. What happens with us? What's next, I mean, in our relationship?"

"I just want it to go back to the night before the play and how we felt afterwards, when we came over here," Joanna said. "I know we can't wipe this episode out of our minds. It did happen, but when I was dancing with you the night before, I couldn't have been happier," she said pulling away from me to look into my eyes. "But then, this woman, this woman posing as someone else comes along and boom, I'm in a world of thugs, drug dealers, and fearing for my life. Not exactly what I was expecting to happen."

"I realize that," I responded. "Branch was evil and I should say still is. She was someone that fooled me in a time of weakness. She had me in her sights for some time. I just can't figure out why. I mean, she knew my first wife long after I had divorced. She said I didn't pick her, but I never knew who she was then. She knew me and had her eye on me at the time. I just had no idea."

"Well, it really makes me wary that she may still have both of us in her sights. I do really hope they find her and bring her to justice," Joanna said looking distant and thoughtful. "It's my connection to you that puts me in danger. I fear that she is wanting to harm us and that no matter where we go, she will find us. I don't know if we can take much more of these episodes and not have it ruin us. I wish we could run away somewhere and never be found."

"I get it, Joanna. She is the one thing that will truly stand in our way of having what we want for us. I guess I am being hopeful, thinking that you will want to stay in this relationship. I understand all that you are thinking and we have so much to discuss, but please, at least say that you will give it a few days of thought. Maybe then discuss how we feel about us," I said, cringing on the inside as I didn't want to spend any days apart.

Joanna turned towards me and I felt a sudden twinge of anticipation that she was about to say something I didn't want to hear.

"Mike, I really can't imagine spending any more days apart," she said as I saw her eyes beginning to fill with tears that she was trying to hold back. "When I first met you, I didn't know what to think. You seemed a bit too arrogant and I wasn't sure if I was reading you right. I know we don't know each other as well as we should, but I do want to know you better and I hope that you feel the same. I'm in love with you and I am quite sure of that. But, if we are to get farther in our relationship, there are things we have to know about each other and our pasts. I want you to be able to tell me all you decide you should tell me, but I also don't want to find out something later that I wish I had known earlier. I hope that makes sense. We need to be honest about our past to be good for each other in the future."

"I certainly understand that," I said looking directly at her. "We will do that. I promise I will tell you my story, but, please, know that I do love you and that all I will tell you is to help us go forward. Everything I tell you will not be something I am proud of or would like you to hear. It's just letting you know who I am, and what I want to be for you, for me, and for us."

We had decided at this moment to take the next step in relationships, which would open up a box of memories, some that I didn't want to come out. Some of it would be painful, some of it pitiful, but, for us, honesty and openness would be the only thing that would create us as a couple. Right now, from this point on, we would walk a slow and cautious path to either building this relationship up or tearing it down. I think I knew what we both wanted. Surviving the truth, navigating our past, and bringing it up to speed was our intention. How that was going to either begin us or end us was the question that we did not know how to answer. We just had to open the box and find out.

CHAPTER 3

Andy Marx was still in Florida. His Tuesday would be pretty much filled with the questioning of Carrianne Martinez. Carrianne was hopefully going to be the witness they would need to go after the cartel. He showered, dressed, and headed down to the hotel lobby to get a coffee before he headed on to the interview downtown.

He had wondered, most of the night, what her approach to being this star witness would be. He had a list of questions that he wanted to ask. He had a strategy that he hoped would lead to the destruction of the cartel and bring Allison Branch to justice. He dealt with his own thoughts of how and when he would come face to face with her again. He didn't fear her, but, again, he was cautious. Evil had its way when it was set loose and he was going to be careful and not take her for granted. She had escaped the last time, but this time, it would be the last showdown. Andy knew that the next encounter would be the end for

Allison. He would make sure of it.

He took the coffee and headed to the front of the hotel and caught a cab for downtown. Today, he would meet with FBI agents, Paul Chrisler and Jenna Holmes, before questioning Carrianne to see what they knew. They both had been instrumental in the chase that pinned Branch down in Miami-Dade County, Florida. They had almost succeeded in her capture, but due to a bomber, she had gotten away. Andy was going to leave no stone unturned in his quest to hunt Branch down.

On the ride to the police station, Andy picked up his phone and punched in Katy O'Neal's number. He was about to push the call button but just stared at it. He had thought of her last night and wondered why he was taken by her. She was really not quite his type, but yet, he felt some sort of attraction to her. He had a few dates before and mostly his type was the strong, independent woman. Yet, she was very much on his mind. He stared at the number and then finally closed it and put it back in his pocket. He couldn't make the call. He had way too much to deal with at the moment. Maybe he would try later.

▲

Katy O'Neal was home again and wishing she would hear from Andy Marx. During her time at the hospital after the incident, she had been impressed with his good looks and his confident manner. He came across to her as that strong man that she would need to counter her weaknesses. Katy also wanted to be independent and strong. God, how she wished she was strong. Every time she felt that she was finding her stride, something would cause her to retreat into 'poor little Katy'. She needed to be in charge of her life, not let her life throw her around like a rag doll.

Today, she was trying to put back the pieces of her life into something that made sense to her. She was trying to recall all that had happened to her and it was all mostly because she knew Mike Parsons. Mike was the man she so desperately wanted to pay attention to her. He was the one she was hung up on and needed to love her. He couldn't or wouldn't and it was not due to her lack of effort. It was still her conflict when she thought of another man. She wanted to let him go, wanted to make Mike something in her past, not this lingering thought that kept showing up in her daydreams.

I was a bartender and bartenders didn't get involved with characters like Allison Branch, Breanne Jackson, and drug cartels. At least, I never thought so. My job wasn't supposed to cause my kidnapping. Not once, but twice! I just have to recover from this. I have to be better. I just wish Marx would call, I really want to talk to him. I just know he will turn me down, just like Mike did. He will see me for what I am. I have to change, I have to be stronger. I wasn't strong enough for Mike, and I am not going to make that mistake again. Mike has someone else, but why didn't he want me?

Katy's thoughts were interrupted by a knock on her door. She froze momentarily as she wondered who it could be. She instantly thought of Branch and the cartel and was paralyzed in her chair. The knock came again and slowly, she got out of her chair and went to look out the peep hole and saw that it was Nick, her boss at O'Shea's. She finally breathed out all the air she held inside and opened the door for him.

"Come in, Nick," Katy said as they went to the living room. "Things have been crazy as you know and I want to get back to work as soon as possible. I was wondering about maybe in a couple of days?"

"Take as long as you need. The place hasn't been the same without you, but I have you covered until you feel ready to come back," Nick said sitting in the chair across from Katy.

"Thanks, Nick. I want to be back, but there are a few things to tie up after this latest nightmare. I'll just need a few days," Katie said smiling at Nick.

Nick had always tried to take care of Katy. He was a fatherly image that she had lacked, and he was a great boss to work for. Katy knew that Nick had her back. He could be demanding at work, but he expected a lot from his employees. He had a compassionate side that made them all feel like the restaurant was a good place to be, even though it was work.

"Okay, look, today is Tuesday, why don't we look at Friday as being your first day back?" Nick asked. "I think that gives you time to recover. If you need more, we can stretch it out."

"Nick, that is fine. I am so glad I work for someone like you," Katy responded.

"Katy, I don't mean to pry, but if you want to come and stay with Jessica and me, we have room and maybe you will feel a bit safer."

"Thanks for the offer, Nick, but I think I will be okay. Let's just see how I do the next few days, I really don't want to impose and there are some things that need my attention right now," Katy said, wishing that she had taken him up on this.

"Okay, so, I will see you on Friday around five?" Nick asked.

"Yes, I will be there, and Nick, thanks for offering. I appreciate the fact that you and Jessica would take me in, but I just have to get over all of this and I need to do that on my own," Katy said.

"The offer stands, but I understand. Anytime you

feel unsafe, you are always welcome," Nick said.

Nick got up out of his chair and headed for the door. Katy walked with him and said goodbye and watched him walk down the sidewalk. He turned after a few steps and told her, "Remember, the offer stands."

"Thanks, Nick." Katy felt a bit better and gained some confidence from Nick's visit. She began to feel safer, knowing that she did have a place to go if it was needed. But for now, she was fixed on doing this alone. She had to do this, she had to become strong and independent. She had to change her life. There was this one little thing that she just couldn't get out of her mind. That one thing was the possibility of having to face Allison Branch again someday. She asked herself, *"if she was standing right in front of you, and you had the opportunity, could you pull the trigger? Well, could you?* Funny thing, she never realized that there were others who had asked themselves the same question when it came to Allison Branch. She waved at Nick as he drove away and asked herself again, *"well, could you?"*

CHAPTER 4

The authorities were going to begin the investigation as soon as they possibly could. Carrianne Martinez was the star witness and information source they would need to hunt the members of the cartel and Allison Branch. Carrianne was led to a room for questioning. Paul Chrisler, Jenna Holmes, and Andy Marx were in there along with the US Marshall's escorts that watched the door and hall.

She had dreaded this moment, one of betrayal and shame. Yet, she knew it was her only way to someday marry, someday have children. In this process, she would lose her family and never see them again. She thought long and hard and came to this conclusion. She could not turn back now.

Andy Marx started the conversation:

"Good morning, Ms. Martinez. I want to introduce you to Mr. Chrisler and Ms. Holmes with the FBI and they would like to ask you some questions this morning. I want you to try and recall everything for them the way it happened and tell of the drug business that you were involved in. I would like you to remember that you are bound to the memorandum of understanding that was agreed to by yourself and your intermediary. You may consult your intermediary or lawyer at any time. Do you understand everything I have told you?"

"Yes, Mr. Marx, I do understand."

"Good, then let's have Mr. Chrisler begin the questioning," Marx said moving to a seat at the end of the table.

"Good morning." Chrisler began. My name is Paul Chrisler I will be in charge of the investigation into all activities that you have been involved in. The information that I seek is about each and every character involved and the location or locations that we may need to search to find these people. We need to move as quickly as possible, so speed of this questioning period may get overwhelming. First, try to go back to your first involvement with the cartel and the people you met in the early stages."

"Well, when I was younger, maybe 16 or so, in the slums we knew a man named Andres Montoya. He had been around our family for years. My brother, Julio, who you know as Jake, and me, we loved Andres. He watched over us, protected us from physical harm. He made a promise to my mom to get us into the United States illegally as long as we did some work for him and that work involved creating the drug markets in Midwest cities," she said as she took a sip of water from her cup.

"So, Andres took you to the states and you arranged for dealers to distribute, is that correct?" Chrisler asked.

"Yes, that's right. We were young and blended into

clubs and night life with other young people. We looked for those disadvantaged young people looking to make more money. It was dangerous work, but it was also easy to recruit. Each recruit had to have one meeting with Andres before they were trusted. Each recruit was made aware not to cross Andres. He was intimidating and that made our jobs easier," Carrianne said looking away for a moment. "After a few months, Andres found a helper. She was a cop and she had a couple of friends looking to make some money. She kept the heat off of us and created an environment that was much easier for us to navigate. Her name, of course as you already know, is Allison Branch. Branch's friends could deal and make money and she made quite a bit from the cartel to provide this "safer" environment for us to get drugs in to the inner city," Carrianne said raising her eyes to meet Marx's. She thought this may have hit a nerve in Marx and she saw him shuffle uncomfortably in his seat.

Jenna Holmes cut in. "Tell me more about Branch and her behavior during this time. Did she seem stable?" Holmes asked.

"Well, at first, she was, but then over time she started to change. She became more and more aggressive and more detached from everyday life. Her mind seemed to drift more often. Her world was slowly becoming more of a fantasy and after her imprisonment from the first incident at Mr. Parson's lake house, she went downhill fast," Carrianne recalled.

Marx was feeling these words and was stung on the inside. He had trusted Branch and thought she was a good cop. He remembered finding out all that she had been involved in after that incident and didn't know what he was dealing with all along. He had prided himself on being perceptive and was totally fooled on this one. He had no idea until that day at the lake when all hell broke loose.

Paul Chrisler took over and asked Carrianne, "Could you give us the names of the people we are dealing with and their aliases?"

"Well, first there is the Boss, and we were never allowed to know his name. We just had to call him the Boss. We rarely had any face time with him. Then Andres was next in line as he was the main enforcer. Then there was a man named Oscar Stephenson who had a business connection, his name was Jerry Linhart, that partnered with Allison in the Milwaukee and Chicago drug trade. When Jake told detective Marx that I worked at Stephenson's business when the cartel came in to speak to Oscar, we did that as a way to draw you and Parsons into the case to lure you in as a favor to Branch. She really wanted to kill you and Parsons," she said looking away from Marx.

"We knew of Montoya and had drawn a bead on him. Through surveillance, we have found the names of several of the Boss's associates," Holmes said cutting in. "We pinpointed the grow house and had the place blocked off. If not for the explosion, we would have had them. Who was the one that made that explosion happen?"

"We only knew him as the Chemist. We were not allowed to know him by name. He had always been that valuable to the Boss. I don't know anything about him other than he did the work on that explosion and others before, even to kill rivals," Carrianne said. "He always wore a mask."

"That is all of the people you will deal with. You know who most of them are," Carrianne said as she felt that twinge of heartbreak that came with turning on the cartel, endangering her brother.

Marx had taken his seat during the questioning and

didn't say too much. He then broke in at a slow point. "Can you tell us more about how the cartel works and what the operations are?" he asked.

"Of course, you know how the war on drugs has been militarized in other countries. The increased surveillance of ordinary people doing ordinary things on a daily basis is common. We were child soldiers who were involved in facilitating drug traffic, human trafficking, gambling and prostitution. We were never involved with bribing of politicians, that was left to the boss. The wealth of the cartel bought politicians, judges, police, or whatever they needed to keep business alive. Guns and money were available everywhere," she said as she paused to drink her water. Selling to the Mexican cartels was profitable, as much as our own trafficking in the states."

"How well is the Boss's home guarded with gunmen?" Marx asked. "We know that many of them have hordes of gunmen guarding the place."

"You would almost need the military to get in," she responded. "They are there in Brazil and men with AK 47's guard our own grow houses in the US. You recall the two at the Florida grow house that your men gunned down during your search for Parsons, Katy, and the new girlfriend. There are many of them still around all the local grow houses that supply the cities of Milwaukee and Chicago. Marijuana is the cash crop, of course, but meth, so wildly addictive, was the future. Andres and the Boss, they saw that future. It turned out that was where the money would be."

Andy Marx leaned back in his chair and looked at Chrisler and Holmes. Their faces intent as they wrote the information down. He knew the task was daunting. They may never bring Branch back, as getting to where she was would be near impossible with bought off politicians and no help from foreign authorities. The cartel had long fingers that stretched over many parts of this country and in others. They were all in for the war of their lives if they were ever going to find Branch again. She would also have heavy protection. But Marx did know one thing, he knew she could be drawn out. Allison Branch's ego was way too large to stay hidden for too long. He had to flush her out and end her. He knew there would be that one moment of destiny and he wasn't going to leave it to the FBI. This time would be the last because he knew that he **could** pull the trigger. This would be his last act on the force. He knew he would be done with it, but first, he needed to end Branch. Marx knew the one story about Branch that would make it happen. A story that she never meant to reveal to anyone, but did to Marx one night over a few beers. The questioning continued.

CHAPTER 5

It was Tuesday and Joanna wanted to go home to check on her house. I stayed home and contacted the university to let them know when I was coming back to work. Late spring and early summer were approaching and I was thinking of fishing at the lake. It was always my place to gather my thoughts. It was where I did my best soul searching. I was sure that by June, I could have things sorted out a bit and James, my brother, and I could have some time at the lake to fish.

I also wanted some time there with Joanna. I wanted the lake house to be a special place for her, too. I didn't want it to be just my place, I wanted it to be ours. Funny, how most of my life had never been talking about the concept of "ours" or "we". I had mostly dealt in the world of "me" and "mine". I had struggled so much with other people and my other rough times that were self-induced, that the concept of "us" had totally escaped me.

I told Joanna I was going to school to take care of some loose ends at the office and get back to speed. I told her how to work the alarm system and if she went somewhere, she would have access to protection. I would also be followed by officers to the school. Our lives were really not private right now. There was always protection and would be until this was over, if it ever would be. I hoped that I could somehow return to a normal life. It seemed since 2010, it was nothing close to normal.

Riding in the back of an unmarked was not unfamiliar to me. I had done this before. During the ride to my office, my phone rang and it was Marx.

"Hi, Andy," I said looking around and not wanting to say too much. "I'm on the way to my office to tie up some loose ends. How are things going?"

"Pretty good," he said. "We have gathered a lot of information that is helpful. It is going to be a real tough situation, you know," he said pausing. "This is the most dangerous thing I've ever taken on while in the force. My role is somewhat diminished because the Feds and locals have so much jurisdiction. But, being involved in the previous two incidents gives me some leverage."

"I know you can't talk about it much," I said, feeling uncomfortable around the cops in my presence. "I will talk later, but things are fine here."

"I want to call you later. Don't answer me, but I want to call you later tonight. There are a couple of things I need to talk with you about," Marx said.

"Right," I responded knowing he wanted to keep this quiet.

The car drove on, headed to the university.

Once again, I felt involved. I needed to help Marx not just find HER, but end HER. I knew it was both of our intentions to see it come to a permanent close. It just had to happen and we both knew it for certain. I realized at the moment I hung up the phone, that it would be Marx and me at the end. In whatever scenario that would surely play out, I knew it would be easier to just let the authorities handle it, but if all of our lives were to move forward, my life, Marx's life, Joanna's, Katy's, all of us, then Branch would have to permanently be in the rearview mirror.

"Mike, do you believe in destiny?"

Well, I think I knew the answer to the question Branch had asked me at the Sidecar bar.

"Yes, Allison, I think I do believe in destiny. Even now, more than ever, I believe in destiny."

CHAPTER 6

I got home later that afternoon and Joanna was there waiting for me. I was glad to be home with her. She seemed to be in a pensive mood and not her normal self. I walked to her and kissed her cheek.

"Mike, I was wondering how long it would be before our lives would be back to normal. I think about being captive in that house and I remember one thing much more vividly than anything else. It was that woman, that Allison Branch. Her eyes looked, well, crazy is the right word," she said looking up at me.

"Yes, I know," I said trying to play down the talk.

"Do you think she will ever stop hunting you down?" she asked.

"We can't be sure, but my mind tells me that if they don't find her, and soon, we will see her again," I said taking her hand and leading her to the living room.

We both sat on the couch and I put my arm around her. I only wanted to hold her, to have her lay her head on my chest. I wasn't really in the mood for a conversation about Branch, but it was on Joanna's mind.

"I know this whole thing seems so bizarre to you, but with time, it can slowly pass. We just need to be confident in Marx and the Feds to get this done," I said.

"I'm not so sure," Joanna said looking up at me. "I just can't believe that I really thought she was just this poor girl with a tough past, just looking for a new start. When I hired her, I had no idea of what she was like. She seemed normal, actually.

"Normal, is not what she is. We were both fooled by her. She's a great actress and you saw that first hand," I said remembering her on the stage. "She might have been better than the rest of the kids you had in the play."

"Well, I have to admit, she was good. I just never saw any of that coming," Joanna said looking worried as if the memories of her were starting to bring some fear back into her eyes.

"Look, we are going to move forward. We'll get back to work and the days and weeks will go by, we will have our own relationship to work on, and then after they find her, and I just feel that they will, we will be free to be us. But, in the meantime, we are going to live as normal as we can. Each day is going to get better," I said wanting to convey confidence that I really wasn't feeling on the inside.

"I sure hope so," Joanna whispered softly, "I sure hope so."

I held on to her, wondering if what I said would be actually what would happen. I really didn't have the confidence I wanted to project, but I was not ever going to let Joanna know that. We had a lot invested in each other, in this relationship. I was holding on tight and I wasn't going to let go.

In ending this horrific story, it would have to be one of us. It would surely come down to whether it was me or it was HER. One of us would come to their demise. I really didn't know if I was courageous enough, strong enough, good enough to make it HER demise, but I knew in my heart, it had to be one of us. That was enough to shake me to my core. It would be the cause of many more bad dreams that would stalk me for quite some time.

▲

Allison Branch was needing surgery. It would not be for another two weeks. The doctors that examined her told the Boss that this would take time. The Boss, fearful of the American Feds coming for the cartel, had to find somewhere for this to take place. The Boss, Jake, and the rest of the cartel would have to be on the move. The Feds may find the place, but they would be long gone. He had the right place in mind and they would be moving in a few days. He had to make all the plans and let Jake know what he wanted him to do.

The Boss had grown fond of Branch over time. He was not in love with her by any means. He had plenty of women for his needs. He felt that she was good at what she did and was helpful to the cartel. But with the FBI coming after them, he wondered how smart it was to keep her around. He had played with the idea of eliminating her. It would be easy enough if she was no longer in the picture. He could not decide, but he was thinking it through. Even the thought of faking her death and letting it be known she was gone and cut to pieces had crossed his mind. He had options and he had the people to carry out his plan. All he really knew was he had to decide. Soon.

The doctors had finished the examination and the Boss and Jake had left the room. The doctors followed them to the living area of the posh and spacious home. Dr. Renaldo and Dr. Costa were the two best plastic surgeons the Boss knew.

"We can do this but her healing time will be significant," Dr. Renaldo said. "She may have some scarring, we cannot guarantee, but we can make her look different enough from her old face that she may not be recognized."

"Yes," Dr. Costa added. "It is very possible that she could retain some looks, but it is also possible that scarring would be a side effect. We will need facilities and equipment. It will take some time but she will be back to working for you in a few months."

Jake looked at the Boss who appeared to be thinking deeply about something and the look on the Boss' face was causing him concern.

"You are going to do this, right? Jake asked, hoping he was reading the Boss wrong.

"Yes, Jake, we will do this. We just need another place to go besides here," the Boss responded. "We will all need to go together. Garon and Aberto will accompany us as well. I think I know the right place to go.

Garon and Aberto were the top henchmen in the cartel. They had been with the Boss for a long time and were loyal to him since they were teenagers. Their rise in the cartel was quick and now, in their twenties, they were hardened men, skilled in shooting, fighting, and self-preservation. They had killed and would do so again at any time. They nodded and moved off into the patio area, leaving Jake with the Boss and the doctors.

"I will have everything set up for you," the Boss told

Dr. Renaldo. "I will contact you of the date and time to be there. Let me know what you need and it will be there for you."

"Very well, sir," Dr. Renaldo replied as he and Dr. Costa were ready to leave. The Boss accompanied them to the door.

"I am counting on you both," the Boss said as he opened the door to let them out. Garon and Aberto were standing there on the patio, smoking, weapons carried over their shoulder. "I will be shooting for next Monday if that will fit in your schedule," the Boss said.

"We will be available then," Dr. Costa said. With that they were escorted off the grounds by the two henchmen and would be driven back to the city.

The Boss walked back inside and approached Jake.

"Look, Jake, this woman has been good for the cartel. Can you keep her under control?"

"I am sure I can, sir," Jake replied.

"You have to. I am counting on you to make that happen. She has gone off the rails and needs to be brought back. Whatever it takes, do it. We can't afford careless mistakes. Not with Americans looking for us," the Boss said looking into Jake's eyes. He was looking for a sign of weakness or doubt in Jake. He could find none.

"Count on me," Jake said firmly and decisively. "I understand her and I can control her."

"Good, I am depending on that fact. Don't mess this up, it is crucial to keep her sedated and under supervision. This is much too serious," the Boss said.

The look on the Boss's face bothered Jake. He had seen the look many times with rival cartel bosses and his enemies. He meant what he said and Jake was going to have to protect her. Any slip-ups and it could be the end for her. He walked towards Branch's room. He couldn't stay away too long.

CHAPTER 7

A couple of weeks had passed and I was beginning to get back in the swing of work and having Joanna at home with me in the evenings. I was beginning to love her being there. My life had been so helter-skelter and now I was starting to feel the idea of living with someone was what I really wanted and, in fact, needed.

I was heading home with my police protection ride from work and stopped at the store to get a few things. The officer went with me and still, this irregular part of my life, police protection, would still be part of my everyday routine. Joanna was already home and an officer was there watching our house. I hope that very soon, this would end and Branch would be caught and brought back to justice by the Feds. Our lives just had to be different. We couldn't do this forever.

My phone rang and I could see it was Marx. I started to ignore the ringing, but answered out of my own curiosity.

"Hey, Marx," I said.

"Good afternoon," Marx replied. "Are you with anyone right now?" he asked.

"Well, yeah. Why do you ask?" I returned.

"I don't want you to reply. I don't want the officer to know what I am saying to you. Just answer me with yes or no answers," Marx said, pausing for just a few seconds. "Look, I know you need this break from all the action," he continued. "I don't want an answer yet, but I was wondering about something. I am looking to get off the force soon and we both know what is at stake here. Any chance that you and I go rogue, you know, just me and you hunting her down, drawing her to us?" he asked. "Don't say no yet, just hear me out."

"Uh, I don't know, Marx," I said.

"Wait, just listen to me for a minute," he said. "You and I both know that someday, somehow, Branch is coming back. She hates us that much. Even if we plan to draw her out, she may already be planning something for us. Maybe she is way ahead of us. I don't know how much we can sit back and wait. I just want this to be over and then I can retire from the force and get on with my life, and you can put this in your rear view."

"Yes, I see that," I said careful to not let the officer know what we were talking about.

"I'm not wanting to pin you down right this moment. I am flying back tomorrow and I was wondering if you could meet me sometime in the next few days?" Marx asked.

"Sure," I said hating myself already. I wanted to tell him all the reasons I would say no, but I couldn't with the protection officer walking along side of me in a grocery aisle.

"Listen, I will call you when I get back to town. We can get together and at least talk about it," he said waiting through my long pause.

"Ok, just let me know," I said and hung up. I hated myself for even agreeing to meet. But I knew I would say yes. We both had known for who knows how long, that someday, we would be back in this together.

What would Joanna think. She deserved to be told, but I still had the choice of saying no, didn't I? Geez, I was starting to hate myself already. I would hear Marx out first and then discuss with Joanna. But she'll leave you buddy, you know she will. I want my life with Joanna, but would I ever have it if we don't get rid of Branch? I understand Marx's feelings, but I really can't say what I am willing to give up for this. Not Joanna, I can't give her up. I just know it's not fair to her if I don't say something. The trust we are trying to build will wither if I keep it from her. I needed a few days to think it over. Yeah, I had to frame that conversation in the right way, but I am afraid if I do tell her I might do it, she will leave. Always conflicts in my life. It just never ends...

_____▲_____

Margaret Linhart had never learned to grieve her husband's death. She had never gotten over Sheila's suicide to begin with, but there was also the affair. The affair she had found out that Jerry, her husband had, left her with an inability to mourn for her dead husband. She had in some strange way, let go of him much easier than she did Sheila. It was as if she had wanted him to be gone, to be erased from her life, but without Sheila, and no Jerry, she was all alone. She had no one else, really, and I felt sorry for her.

I had stopped by on many occasions to see if she was okay. We seemed to talk better, maybe better than we ever had. I was going by to see her again, on my way to work one day this week, just to know that she would be safe from her own depression. I had known depression myself and was glad I had a therapist to talk with. I was hoping to do the same for her.

It was Friday and the weekend was here. I wanted to stop by Margaret's, and my protecting officer left me and waited outside in the car. I went to Margaret's door and rang the doorbell. She appeared shortly, still in her robe and slippers. She was beginning to show signs of wear from all that had happened and aging much faster than I remembered. Each time I saw her, it seemed that she sported new wrinkles and age lines. Her eyes were much darker than I remember.

"Please, come in, Mike. It's good to see you," she said wearily.

"Thanks, Margaret," I returned and entered into the hallway.

"Would you like something to drink?" she asked.

"No, thank you. I'm fine," I said, walking towards her kitchen to sit with her briefly. "I really can't stay too long. My protection officer is outside and I don't want him to wait too long. Is everything alright?" I asked almost shocked at her appearance as she sat down slowly at the kitchen table.

"No, not really, Mike. I'm just more tired and am trying to find some meaning in my life. The few friends I have left in my life don't stop by and the only person I have seen lately is you. I saw the terrible incident on the news and it always bring back the memories of Sheila's death. I just can't get over it," she said sounding weak and wistful.

"Have you thought about professional help?" I asked, not wanting to offend her. "I have a few names of professional people that could help."

She didn't answer, but instead was looking out the

window. "Who and what is she? That woman, that Allison Branch, she must be a terrible human being," she mumbled as her voice became increasingly softer.

"Well, yes, she was and is. I understand what you are feeling." I said

"Do you think they will find her?" she asked looking at me with the dark, dreary eyes that were so unlike her.

"I hope so, but for now, can we get you some help?" I asked.

"I don't know, I really don't know if I want to go through all that," she said as she turned to look out of the window once more.

I really felt that she was in bad shape right now and it was my intention to get her help, whether she thought she needed it or not. I had never seen her so detached, so sad and incoherent. I had to get her help. She was slowly drifting off into a world that was very dangerous to herself. I had heard so many times of people just not taking the extra time to help those that were experiencing mental anguish. Untreated, this type of anguish could lead to suicide as it often did when left unchecked.

"Look, I am going back to set up an appointment for you. Please, just let me do that for you. Can you do that sometime next week? It is important to me," I said looking to her hopefully.

"Okay, I suppose," she said. "You know I miss Sheila every day. She brought me so much joy. I just can't seem to handle the fact she is gone. I may never get over this." Tears began to roll down her face. "I'm sorry," she whispered. "I'm just so depressed."

"I know, I know, Margaret. I'll get that appointment for you and I will be by again tomorrow to check on you," I said. "This will get better. You just need someone to talk to. Please call me at home if you need anything, anything at all."

I patted her arm and got up to leave. I hated leaving her sitting there, but I would call as soon as I got home and get her the help she needed. I owed her that much. We walked to the front door and she let me out, telling me she was glad I stopped by.

"Mike, before you go, I just had to tell you one thing. I never accepted the fact that Sheila committed suicide," she said looking up at me with her dark and sullen eyes. "She was unhappy, yes, but she wouldn't take her own life. I was sure of it. I still believe someone killed her."

I didn't know what to say to that. There was never any talk of murder being the end result. But maybe she was right?

"Look, let's work on you first. We can get to those thoughts later," I said. "I will call you when I get an appointment set up."

I waved goodbye from the sidewalk and watched her slowly close the front door. *Geez my life was so dark...Murder? Is that a possibility? Maybe she's not so wrong.*

CHAPTER 8

I got home and my wonderful Joanna made me a drink. We went out to the patio as the day was warm enough to sit outside. The air was still crisp and I never took off my jacket. We sat in our chairs and began to talk about our day. I told her about stopping by Margaret's. I was telling her about how bad she was looking and that maybe we should both try to convince her that she needed counseling and therapy. Joanna wasn't immediately warm to the idea but was willing to give her own therapist a call to see if she could find room in her schedule for her.

I said nothing about Marx's call and while we were talking the thought crossed my mind many times to bring this up. I just couldn't find the right place to begin. When our conversation paused, I didn't bring it up and I hated myself for it, but I convinced myself to wait until I had heard Marx out completely. By my own admission, I was going to keep it from her until after I saw Marx. I began to loathe myself again.

Joanna talked on and I listened carefully, but in the back of my mind, there was always the call I would get from Marx. *"What would I tell him and why can't you just say no? I know it's wrong, and Joanna will tell me to stay out of it. But I somehow know what my answer to Marx would be and I also know that I risked losing Joanna if I didn't tell her now.*

We finished talking and I took my drink back inside. We sat down to a homecooked meal that would have pleased anyone in a restaurant. This lady could cook, too! I looked across at her and told her how great dinner was. She smiled, that smile that made me feel like I was home. So much closer to my redemption and to our happiness, and yet, so very far away. At that moment, I didn't know how far...*Murder? Was Sheila murdered? I can't get that thought out of my mind. Margaret knew something that I didn't.*

▲

Carrianne Martinez had spent three days with the Feds and had told them everything that she knew about her former life and the cartel. Agents Chrisler and Holmes had questioned her thoroughly and had enough leads to get started. She was about to begin her anonymous life as someone else. She had been well disguised as she left the building after her third day of questioning.

Carrianne and her intermediary were now going to their temporary safe place, for the time being, and would soon begin the process of slowly melting into society in some strange town in quiet America. She knew she would exist on her own, starting her life over. The process would be long and would be mentally taxing, but she was ready, ready to go into hiding, knowing that she would always be brought back under cover to testify if the Feds completed their mission.

She had much work to do, to assume a new identity, new ID, new name and new accounts to memorize. She had no idea of where she may be going, but she was ready. She knew now, the only person who would endanger her would be herself. She needed to stay disciplined and not yearn for an old life. If she weakened, it could mean her own death. She had to stay with the plan.

She had no idea how long it would take to adjust to her new world. But for the moment, she was glad to be starting over again. She felt that she had cleansed herself, that she would now at some point begin her new life in the quest for love and happiness and, of course, the motherhood she had always dreamed of.

_____▲_____

The surgery had been completed by Dr. Renaldo and Dr. Costa. The process had taken many hours but it was the second day of recovery for Allison Branch. This time, her recovery may be slower, but with no guarantee of restoring her beauty and the way her eyes worked for her.

Jake had been there the whole time and was sitting by her bed as she awakened from her drowsy, medication- induced sleep.

As she slowly peered out of her sleepiness, she had noticed her vision being blurry, but her focus was on the image to her left. He came into focus and she knew right away it was Jake.

"Jake, I'm so glad you are here," she said, her voice creaking from the effects of the anesthetic. These days seem like months. I just want to be me again."

"You need to rest and not talk for right now. The doctors did a very good job, and soon, you will be back to feeling better," Jake said reach out to touch her shoulder. He got out of his chair and stroked her left arm to comfort her.

"What do you know, I mean about how well they did?" she asked.

"They didn't talk much to me. They gave the Boss the most information and he hasn't spoken to me about it yet," Jake said still rubbing her arm. "Look, you're going to be fine, you had the best doctors that you could have possibly had. I am sure they did the very best they could."

The 'very best they could' would not be enough. I was always very pretty and it was my asset. I will be pretty again, I know. When I get to see my face, I will be as pretty as always. They had done it before, right? Jake wouldn't lie to me, would he?

"Jake, you have been so good to take care of me. I know you have been there all along. You wouldn't be keeping anything from me, would you?" Branch asked.

"No, Allison. I wouldn't do that. I know very little. What I do know, I would always let you know," he said patting her leg. "In the next few days you should be able to get up and around a bit. But it will take weeks before the doctors will allow you to even look at your face. There is much healing left to do."

"Jake, would you please come see me every day?" she asked, knowing Jake was her closest ally.

"Sure, of course, I will. Right now, you just need rest and quiet. We will talk later. Right now, I have a meeting with the Boss and maybe he can tell me more about what the doctors said. Get some rest and I will be back before you know it," Jake said as he got up to leave the room.

Here we go again, Allison. Fight for everything in your life. Never a dull moment since the day that so-called dad of yours walked out of your life. I will heal, I will get out of here soon. Rest and quiet, my ass. What I need is revenge. I need to get up and around because I have work to do. My story doesn't end here in South America. And when I heal, I had better be just as pretty. If not, then there will be hell to pay. I will be pretty again, won't I? Sure, I will. Of course, you will, Allison...

With that, Allison drifted back to sleep.

Allison's dream was like many others she had had in her life. It always began with the drunk father and him abusing her mother and ended in tragedy. He left, as always in all her dreams, and she cried, just like before. Her mother would take her hand and off they went for their drive to Downers Grove. To the park and the children's area, the only place she ever went that made her feel like a girl, loved, appreciated, and happy in a place where nature healed her. The water of the small pond, the grass waving in the wind, her mother laughing and watching her smell the flowers, and there were the trees. Yes, the trees at Downers Grove were beautiful and they were all Allison's trees. She loved them and she loved her mother. She would have a reoccurring nightmare that always ended up the same. Her mother had disappeared and Allison would look all over Downers Grove for her. She wasn't there. She ran around in a panic, crying, "Mommy, Mommy, where are you?" She would begin to scream out of fear that her father had done something bad to her mother, crying out, "somebody help me find my mom!" Tears and more tears, always tears. She ran through the grass, towards the pond that was her favorite place. There she stopped in her tracks and there her mother was, floating still and face down in the water, in the pond at Downers Grove. She screamed and screamed until the screams began to be real as she woke from her sleep.

The Downers Grove dream would always make her scream...and Andy Marx knew why.

CHAPTER 9

Marx was flying home and he was needing to get back to the office and catch up his work in the department. It was work he was debating whether or not to continue. He had seen a lot in his young and decorated career. He leaned back in his seat and closed his eyes. He needed rest and he was beginning to feel dejected about this case. There were stacks of papers and files on his desk. He was so far behind. He could never seem to end the merry-go-round. He knew it was HER that drove him to his thoughts. It was HER that was causing all this anguish for him and for others. He wanted to end HER, but she was actually ending him, slowly but surely, he had become more despondent about the work he was doing.

He had tried to uphold his oath for truth, justice, and all that he was brought up to think was right. His trust in his own values was beginning to wear down and the bad guys were winning. You could only do so much, he thought, but they were out there, in large numbers, like an army that kept coming at you in waves, no matter how many you eliminated. The new crooks kept taking their place. He could only take down so many. There was only one more in his mind that he needed to take down. It was the one who took the same oath that he did, his ex-partner who had gone off the deep end, that he now was focused on. If he had to play by the rules, Allison would escape again. Prison is not the answer. If he couldn't bring her to justice, he would have to bring justice to her.

This mental ping pong game had gone on his mind ever since the Florida incident. He knew exactly what he wanted to do, but it would take something very extraordinary for him to complete the task. He felt he needed to do something different, but he didn't really know anything else except this life he had dedicated himself to for years. He only knew how to be a cop, and he was damn good at it.

His mother and father so much wanted him to find a nice girl and have a family. He had not thought of bringing someone else in his world to go through the same horrors that he lived through every day. He didn't think he needed to worry a spouse and he felt that no one deserved those sleepless nights, waiting and wondering if their husband would be home that night, or if he would live through the night. He just never had found that special someone. He thought he was getting too old to have that happen. That part of his life was going to pass him by.

Those thoughts had brought Katy back to his mind once again. He remembered almost calling her, but how he had chickened out at the last minute. He would call when he got back, he thought, just to check on her. Somehow, he knew in his mind that it would be more than that, more than just checking up on her.

But for a man so steady and sure of himself, a confident man, almost cocky to a point, he wasn't so sure about Katy. He wasn't so sure about his job, his life, or where he was actually headed. But there was something about Katy that made him pause. He couldn't put his finger on it, but maybe, just maybe, she was like a gift he refused to take. Why not, she had appeared to him through this crisis, but was she really **that** woman? That one chance in a lifetime to find what he so desperately needed?

He would call when he got back, yes, this time he wouldn't just look at the number, he would push the call button. He fell asleep and awoke that morning back home in Milwaukee. He needed to make two phone calls. One would be to his friend, Mike Parsons. The other call he hoped he could make was to Katy O'Neal. But first he had to call Mike...

◢

The first call to Mike was easy to make but hard for Marx to find the right words to hopefully inform Mike of what may happen and how they could deal with it. Andy Marx had decided to take some of his accumulated sick leave to bring an end to Allison Branch, his last official duty as a cop. When she was done, then he would retire from this line of work. No more chases, no more gunfights, no more killers. Then maybe he could settle down and find someone to share a real life with. He was smart enough to go back to school and change career paths. He needed the change. But for one more time, he needed to be at his absolute best.

My phone rang and I looked to see who it was. It was Andy Marx. I cringed because I hadn't discussed any of this with Joanna yet. My penchant for putting off the inevitable once again put me in an "in the moment" scenario.

"Hey, Andy, how are things going?" I asked.

"Going well," he said. "Remember our conversation today? I am going to ask you if you could do this call private."

"Sure, but remember, I haven't agreed to anything and Joanna doesn't know," I said as I made sure she was engrossed in her television show. I walked onto the patio and quietly shut the door behind me. I feel like I am making progress in a relationship for maybe the first time in my life.

"Just hear me out. You don't have to tell her anything yet. Just find some time to swing by. It will take a few months to get it together. Then we can get this over with. Who knows, maybe the Feds will get her before that. But what do you want Branch to be able to do? Maybe she can come back and kidnap Katy, Joanna and you again, maybe kill all of us. You know she is capable of doing that," he said in a voice that was firm and decisive.

"Man, I don't know," I hesitated, feeling my allegiance torn between Marx and staying in this relationship.

"C'mon, look, we can do this. I know it won't be easy, but listen, I think you know it is HER or us. We get her before she gets us. Don't you think she's already planning our demise? If she's hurt bad enough, and doesn't regain her looks, she's going to go off like a time bomb. You know she will," Andy said.

I sat in silence for seconds before replying...

"Okay, look, I'll swing by your place tomorrow, but get my protection cleared. I really don't want Joanna to know what I am doing. Not right now," I said, already beginning to realize what I was saying. I was actually considering working with Marx on this again.

What is wrong with me? I know I don't have to say yes to this. I already hate me, once again! "Okay, Marx, we'll talk about it. See you tomorrow."

I hung up and turned to walk inside. I opened the door and saw Joanna making a coffee in the kitchen. She was pretty, I stood there frozen in a brief moment of self-loathing and fear. *I have to tell her, I just had to. This wonderful woman will walk away from you in a heartbeat if you do this. You know she will.*

"Mike, who was on the phone?" she asked.

"Just Marx, he was just getting back to town." I replied.

"Oh, did he fill you in on what's going on?" she asked, peering at me with a quizzical look.

"Uh, yeah, just letting me know how it went with the Martinez girl," I said looking away.

"Mike, you're not going to get involved with this again, are you?"

Truth, Truth, better than a shallow lie.

I could feel my face getting hot, like that one embarrassing moment you're caught with your hand in the cookie jar.

"No," I said trying to make eye contact. "I told him I wasn't interested in putting us in that situation."

Half-truth. Damn it.

"I think that she is dangerous. Getting involved in this again will only put us both in danger once more," she said with commitment in her eyes. "It's just something that the authorities have to do. For us, we need to work on making our lives better."

But not getting involved may get us killed, too.

"You don't have anything to worry about. Things will work out for us. They just have to," I said, taking the coffee cup from her hand and holding her. She laid her head on my chest, stroking the side of my cheek with her hand. I was coming to a moment. One in which I had to call myself out one way or another. Like many moments like this that we all have, we put off the truth too long. I was putting this off and beginning to hate myself once again.

I would talk to Marx first. Right, talk to him first and see what he is thinking. If I don't like it, Joanna and I never have that conversation. Just one more day, right? What could it hurt? Trying to find a way around it again, aren't you? Keep it to yourself, just one more day. One more day. But you know she'll leave you. You know it. They all leave you.

I called Andy the next day and had him come to my office. It was the safest way to have this conversation. I didn't want to go behind Joanna's back, but it felt like I was. I only wanted to hear him out and then decide what Joanna and I would need to discuss, if anything.

He came in dressed casually and looking tired. He had been through a lot and he was showing signs of wear and tear. He was not the cocky partner of Allison Branch anymore. He had aged from these incidents and he didn't look as young as he used to.

"Come on in, Andy. It is good to see you. I hope you don't mind coming here, but the office leaves me more to myself here," I said while shaking his hand. "Have a seat."

"Thanks for seeing me, Mike. It has been a busy past few days and I am glad to be back in Milwaukee," Marx said as he sat across from me in one of the chairs across from my desk. His eyes were looking weary and I knew he was about to drop something on me.

"How is Carrianne doing?" I asked.

"Pretty good. She is under the WITSEC program and is secure. It was a rough couple of days of questioning for her. I kind of felt sorry for her, but her new life awaits and I think she probably wanted out anyway," Marx said. "The FBI at least knows what and who they are looking for.

"How are you doing?" I asked looking intently at him, searching for a mood that he was in or what he had in mind.

"I'm okay, but not really, if you know what I mean. I want to say I am okay, but there are many things bothering me right now. I'm thinking about getting off the force. This thing has worn me out and I have to get away from all this violence. I wish it was over," he said looking out my window.

The look in his eyes was far away. It was as if he had something planned but wasn't finding the right words to let me know what he had in mind. It scared me that he already had a plan and I was fearing that I would commit to take a part in it. What worried me more was the look that I had seen before looking in to a mirror before I shaved. It was the look of someone that was not happy, someone feeling the depression of not liking his life, and I knew it. I had seen that look before. It was a look I had never seen on Marx. He didn't wear it well.

"Look, I've been there. I understand the very things you are thinking," I said, trying my best to not be too intrusive. "This thing, this Branch thing, it's eating at you and maybe you just need to let it go. Move forward and try to put her out of your mind."

"And, you have?" he asked looking at me as though he knew my answer.

"Well, no, not really. But maybe we just need to give the Feds some time and they will crack this case. We stay out of it and we both get a whole lot better.

Get on with our lives and get this nightmare behind us," I said, hoping he would agree.

'We both know what needs to happen," he said tightening his jaw like he was angry. "You know that we will have to run into her one more time. She's evil and the sooner we get to the end of this story, the better. But the question is, whether it's me or you that does it, one of us has to pull that trigger."

"Look, I don't want to do this again, Marx. I don't know if Joanna will even stay if I say yes to whatever plan you have. I really don't want to lose her. She's made my life better," I said knowing she would do exactly that if I got involved.

"But you can lose her, Mike, if we do nothing. The list of people she wants to kill is getting longer. You know that Joanna is on that list. You can't deny that. Then there's me, Katy, even your brother, James. She's coming back here and you know it," Marx said with a bit more fire than he started out with when he first came into the office.

I was trying to keep that thought out of my head. Branch coming back here to finish us off had always been on my mind. I put nothing past her. But I was having trouble even wanting to ask what he had planned. I didn't want to look scared, but this had real life implications that I had already experienced because I wasn't trained to do this. I didn't think like a cop, fight like a cop, or even have any authority to do anything like this, whatever it was.

"Okay, listen, I'll hear you out. But I won't guarantee that I will say yes," I said almost knowing it was a weak response.

"Alright, here is what I propose that we do..."

CHAPTER 10

When I left for home in a haze, I knew that this was going to cause me much trouble, but, somehow, I could not say no. Why? It was time to tell Joanna. I couldn't keep this from her any longer. It was do or die time. I had dreaded this moment for weeks now. The moment of truth was at hand. As I parked and walked up to my place, I was preparing what to say to Joanna.

I put the key in the door and opened it. I shut off the alarm system. *Why was the alarm set? Oh no!* I called out her name and received no answer. "Joanna, are you here?" No answer. I walked around the place and realized that she wasn't home. As I went to the kitchen to rehearse what to say once more, I found the note.

Mike,

These words are difficult, but I just can't do this anymore. I called your office and the secretary said you were with a detective. I just knew it was Marx and that you were getting involved again. You lied to me and kept that from me. We just can't do that and survive this relationship. I am moving back home and I think I am done with us. I just can't go through that again.

Joanna

I sat and stared long and hard at the note. I had become dizzy somewhat and my skin felt needle-like pricks. I sat on the couch and slumped, feeling once again that my world was caving in all around me. The sinking heart, the self-loathing, and the fear and anxiety felt like I was carrying a load of bricks.

This can't be. I had been trying so hard to recover my life and now it was crumbling once again. What am I missing? This soul of mine, so lost and so desperately needing to heal, was once again shattered.

I picked up my jacket and got my keys. I was headed to O'Shea's, a place where I knew how to defeat my demons, if only for a few hours. A drink, or two or three, would give me relief. It was all I knew.

I was already hating myself. I started the car and pulled out of the driveway.

Here we go again...

▲

I strolled up to the front door of O'Shea's and pulled on the handle to open the door. It wasn't crowded today and, for me, that was good. I had thought that Katy might be there and that she and I could have some sort of cleansing conversation about my new issue. But when I got to the bar, there was a guy working. Oh well, probably it was for the best anyway.

I took my place on the bar stool I usually sat on and

ordered a beer. The guy was nice enough, but as any good bartender could see, I just needed to be by myself. He set the beer down and said, "I'll just start a tab for you."

"Thanks," I said and started to sip on the ice-cold beer and tried to recall all the good things that happened with Joanna and me. We had many good times, but the thought of her kept taking me back to the ugly scenes, the kidnapping, the beatings, and the drugs. I should have left her alone after the first date. She should have never been involved in all of this in the first place. I can't really blame her for leaving. *I just should have been honest with her and just told Marx no. I wouldn't be sitting here right now and she would have still been at my home.*

I finished the beer and then decided it was too weak. A scotch and water would have been better. I waved at the bartender and he came over.

"How about a scotch and water, my friend?" I said.

"Sure thing, I'll get you one," he said going to the whiskey shelf. He poured me one and walked over to set it in front of me.

"Thanks, my friend," I said and took a long sip. I stirred the ice in the drink and thought back to Branch and how she had survived all of this. *SHE was my problem, the one that put me in this situation. Branch just had to come back into my life a second time and ruin a relationship that could actually have healed Joanna and me. SHE just couldn't be stopped and I am afraid that she will waltz right into my life again. "If you had to pull that trigger, could you, well, could you?*

"Hello, stranger," a soft voice over my left shoulder said. "Anyone sitting here?" she asked.

I already knew who it was without looking. I recognized that soft and quiet voice. I turned and saw exactly who I thought it was, Katy O'Neal.

"Oh, Katy, how are you? It's really good to see you. No, no one is sitting there. Pull up a chair and have a drink with me," I said,

"Where is Joanna?" she asked with a puzzled look.

"It's a long story," I said, sipping another large swallow of scotch.

"Why don't you give it a try, you know I will listen?" Katie said.

"I can't, not right now. I just haven't processed it. She left me, just left a note. I haven't talked to her since I read it," I said and swirling my glass of scotch around the cubes of ice. "She realized I had talked to Marx about Branch and I didn't tell her. I thought about it, but I just told Marx I would listen, but made no promise to help him. She called me at the office and found out I was talking to him. I should have told her. I messed up and once again, I am back to where I started," I said looking away.

I looked back at Katy and the look on her face was so different than any I had seen from her before. Her eyes were focused on me. Her concern was genuine, real, it wasn't the old bright, cheerful look that we had as friends. It was more the look that your therapist gave you when they felt you were close to the edge. She had sensed something about me that was dangerous, not to her, but to myself. It was dangerous.

"You can come over, you know. Maybe another setting will give you that chance to talk it out. Do you want to come over?" she asked.

"I can't do that right now, I have to call her. I have to talk to her," I said, sounding weak and pitiful.

Katy's heart sunk a little as she was sure that this was the time, that it was her only chance to have Mike back in her life.

"Well, you know where I am at if you need me," she

said as she got off the bar stool and grabbed her purse and jacket. "Why don't you let me at least give you a ride home?" she asked.

"I'll be fine here, but thanks," I said with a forced smile.

Katy leaned over and kissed me on the cheek. "You know where I live and you have my number."

"I know, but right now I just want to stay here and have a few more. There is just a lot for me to think about," I said. "I do appreciate your offer, but I have to try to talk to Joanna first before I even can make any sense of this. Take care of yourself and I'll be okay here. We'll talk again, soon. Thanks for caring."

She walked back behind the bar and said something to the bartender and then waved as she turned to walk out of O'Sheas. Once again, I let Katy walk. I couldn't, shouldn't. She just didn't need this and neither did I. It was better that I said no.

And here I was. Once again feeling the deep pang that pity and self-loathing can bring. Katy was good, kind, and wanted to help. But here I sat, letting her walk away disappointed and aching. I had wondered for so long, "why not Katy", but always, damn near every time, I shut her out. Not out of anger or something I did or didn't like about her. It was just that I had protected her from me. Always, it was the right thing to do, but was it right now? I think I'll just stay right here and drink. I just can't think right now. I have to get out of here. I know what happens when I stay too long or drink too much. It never ends well.

I waved the bartender over. "I'll take another one when you get a chance," I said.

"Sure thing," he said and walked off to fix another scotch on the rocks.

Oh, here I go again. Fix the pain, the anger, the fear. Yes, this will fix it and it will all go away.

Joanna, Katy, Marx, and HER. Yes, HER. Not one day goes by where I am not haunted by HER. But you know what, Mike? She's somewhere, most likely alive, and most likely coming to get you, get all of us. It would only be a matter of time. Why was I so stupid?

"But if it happens, you meet her face to face...could you pull the trigger...well, could you?

CHAPTER 11

I was dreaming once again. The two little men on my shoulder were having another debate. The one on the left was saying that Allison Branch was surely going to come back to get me. The one on the right was saying that she would be dead soon and there would be nothing more to worry about. The little man on my left shoulder had me convinced that yes, she would be back, but where and how? The one on the right then disappeared and I was left speaking to the evil one.

"She can't come back," I said as I had sweat begin to form on my forehead.

"Here, let me show you," as the little guy made a scene appear before me.

In a dream I could see her. I took a few steps closer. "Allison, Allison! What happened to you? What happened to us?" I asked.

Suddenly, she jumped to her feet at lightning speed and pointed a gun at me, calling out, "Not one more

step or you're dead!"
*Then I saw the eyes, furious and steel blue. The
eyes I had always remembered, but it wasn't Allison.
She looked so made up, almost plastic as her face
was a face I could not recognize. This couldn't be her.
"Allison, please put the gun down. Let me help you.
We can stop this now and we can get you help,
please," I said only hoping she could resist pulling the
trigger.*
*She took one more step closer and fired. The gun
sounded like a cannon, but it didn't hit me...*
Mike, Mike, wake up!...

I sat up in the bed quickly and my head felt like
someone had hit me with a brick. I raised both hands
to my head and tried to focus my vision. Where was I?

Startled I saw someone sitting next to me and she
reached over and touched my shoulder lightly.

"Mike, you had a bad dream. It's going to be okay.
Mike, do you hear me?" she asked.

"Katy, it's you. Where am I?" I asked trying to
shake what I knew was a bad case of the drinking
cobwebs.

"You passed out in the bar. Steve, the bartender
called me and he brought you here. You couldn't drive
and I told him to bring you here. It's 10:00 am and
you were having a bad dream. I could hear you from
the other room. It has to be HER that you are
dreaming about. Why don't you just open up to me?"
she asked.

"Right now, I'm embarrassed. I was just in another
world yesterday. Things are crashing down fast. I'm
just confused. I'm at the rock bottom of the mountain,
looking up again."

"Why don't you shower and I'll fix you some
coffee?" she asked, patting me on my cheek. "You
need to just sit for a bit before you go anywhere. I'll

get you some fresh towels and I'll go brew the coffee."

"Okay, sure, Katy. Thanks for the safe place. I owe you."

Katy left the room and closed the door. I ambled off to the shower and my head was pounding on every step I took. Katy opened the bathroom door and set the towels on the floor letting me know where they were. The shower was helping, but I would have a long day trying to recover.

How ironic that Katy and I had switched roles. She was the one trying to be strong and help me. I had changed in just a couple of days! Two days and I was sinking back to the same old outlook on life. I was crashing fast and what could possibly hold me up? Katy? No, forget it Mike. It's not going to be her. It has to be you, only you and some other power can do this. It might be beyond you, beyond Katy. Do I have enough faith in myself and a higher power to help bring me to redemption?

I finished my shower and dried off. I didn't answer my self-questioning. I just got dressed and headed to the kitchen to have that cup of coffee that Katy had promised. A familiar face, a friend, stood smiling at me. It was a start. At least I was out of that nightmare and back to grim reality.

"Here's that coffee, Mike," she said as she offered me the couch in the living room.

I sat down and sipped my coffee and the drinks from the night before made it taste bitter. The heat from the coffee was good on my throat. The bitterness did not set well on my stomach. *See, drinking is not the answer. You just end up feeling like shit for two days and not solving anything.*

"Thanks for the coffee, young lady," I said in a voice so hoarse it sounded like a croaking frog. "I really must have hit it hard last night. Thanks for the safe haven. I know you have my back, but I really don't deserve that."

"Look, we have always been friends and that's what friends do. It's no big deal. I'm just glad you're safe," she said through her look that was between pity and concern. "Do you want to talk?"

"I don't know. I just haven't processed all that the past few hours have been about. One day, I talk to Marx, Joanna finds out and leaves. The next day I'm drinking coffee here after tying one on. There's just a lot to go through before I'm ready for that," I said looking down at the floor. "I have to try to reach Joanna. I need to see her. Surely I can convince her that I won't work with Marx on this and that I can keep that promise."

"Mike, can you?" Katy asked. "Do you really think you can forget this and just let Marx handle it. I know you, maybe better than anyone. You won't let it go. It's just not who you are."

"Katy, look, I have got to get my life in order. There is not much left for me to do, but try and get Joanna back," I said. "This may not be over with Branch, but I surely don't want to make Joanna feel that involving myself with Branch again is more important to me than she is."

Katy looked sad, but she quickly recovered. Her inner strength had been building since the last incident and she wasn't about to beg or to be weak again. "Mike, you can try. You probably should go try to see her. Tell her you owed it to Marx to hear him out. Just explain. It will be okay."

"Look, Katy, I need to go see Joanna. Thanks for the coffee and a place to stay. I'm sorry, we'll talk later, I promise. I stood up and kissed her on the cheek. "Can you take me to my car?" I asked.

"Sure, sure I can," she said gathering up her coat

and keys. "Let me know how things go. I'm always here when you need me."

At that moment I felt awful. Here was my life saver, bailing me out, and I was wanting to rush off to Joanna. I had to convince her we could still make it. There stood Katy, strong, no tears, just helping me out. She wasn't about to show what might have been in her heart. I was getting worse, she was getting better. I suddenly saw her quite differently. It confused me, but the feeling was not like before. Something different, much different...

▲

It had been a few weeks after surgery and Allison Branch was about to see, for the first time, what her new look would be. She had been bandaged for a couple of weeks and she desperately wanted to see the doctor's work. She had been up and walking around for a few days now, and she did not have much pain. It was quiet except for the dark music she had playing on the speakers in her room. Dark music was her motivator.

Jake was in the other room, and she didn't want hm to look with her. She moved closer to the door and closed it quietly. In her heart there was a deep well of anticipation. Unlike before, she wasn't as excited because she was afraid of what she might see. She had lived confidently for so long, but she put the fear away quickly. She walked closer to the mirror and saw her bandaged image in front of her. She reached up to touch the bandages so that she could unroll them. She unrolled the first two wraps and suddenly stopped. She had a flash back to the explosion and the death of her friend, Andres. She began to grow angry, thinking of Marx, Mike, and that stupid new girlfriend of his.

She finished the first layer and held the cloth in her hands. She began to grip the cloth with both hands, clenched it hard in her fists. *I wouldn't even be doing this again if not for those people. They should have been dead already, but they managed to escape, not once but twice!* She unrolled the cloth and began to tear it in half. Her knuckles were white with fury and the cloth split into two pieces. She dropped it on the floor. *It's still in me, the anger, the pain, the feeling that no one wants me, needs me, but I'll fix it! Yes! I will fix them all.* She dropped the bandages on the floor as her head was beginning to spin. She grabbed the edge of the dresser to steady herself. *Stop it! Just get a grip.* Allison opened her eyes and tried to focus on the task of removing the rest of the bandages. She unwrapped faster and with more confidence.

She had one more layer to take off her face. Her anticipation was about to end. Allison thought of calling for Jake, to have him steady her, but she wanted to do this herself. Her gut was telling her that something was wrong, that she shouldn't finish this chore. She finally talked herself into finishing the last wrap. Slowly it came off, a little skin revealed with each roll. The first part where her scalp met her forehead seemed okay. She continued to roll the bandages off. She just wanted to finish quickly but she couldn't because her inner voice was saying; *Something is wrong, something is not right.* She had made it past her eyes and they were still steel blue and undamaged. It encouraged her that things would be just fine. She closed her eyes and finished unwrapping the last of the coverings as she turned away from the mirror. She froze for just a second or two and took a deep breath. She turned to look.

The screams were piercing. "Jake!! Oh my god! Jake! No, no, nooooo!!"

Jake came running into the room and was frozen on the spot. Her looks were marred by burn scars on each side of her face. Allison was shaking violently and Jake finally moved to hold her. She tried to break away from Jake. She was strong and hard to hold.

"Easy, it's okay," Jake said as he led her towards the bed. "It's going to be all right, I'll get the doctor here and we can do something to fix it, they can, I'm sure."

He held on until Aberto and Garon came running in when they heard the screams. They stood at the door ready to help Jake.

"Aberto, get the shot, now!" Jake exclaimed as he held on. Allison was almost hysterical. There was no way of comforting her except to put her out. He could then get things in order to help her. Aberto came in with the needle and Jake held her steady as he plunged the needle into her arm. Jake felt her body begin to relax. He was able to lay her down as she mumbled something Jake could not understand. He leaned in closer to hear what her lips were whispering. "I'll kill them all. All of them, I will kill them all," she mumbled.

Anastasia, would be asked to testify in the Carrianne Martinez trial and be given immunity for her testimony. She had weighed this in her mind and was supposed to go in to meet with the FBI agents Paul Chrisler and Jenna Holmes. Her mother, still dying and in need of money for treatment, was on her mind also. She could run and try to help the cartel. *Would it be worth it? How much would I make? I would have to run to make it happen. I know where the money is that Andres left, and I would have to make a call, but yes, I would need to run and once I made that choice, there would be no turning back. I only needed to make one call. My mother would get the best treatment, but would I ever see her again?*

She wrestled with her thoughts as she looked down at the letter one more time from the man with whom she had often been romantic. She remembered his dark eyes, his fit body. He cared for her, even though she was only a prostitute. Anastasia never felt worthy of love, she had been with so many men. He just made her feel different. He made her feel safe and safe was something she never really could feel in the midst of her double- dealing life. It was always dangerous and safety was something not in her everyday vocabulary. There were only two people in the world that made her feel safe, her mother and Andres.

She unlocked her phone and stared long at the number. Anastasia had a plan, but she needed others to make it work. If she dialed the number, there would be no turning back. She had an offer to make, and it included a few people. But first, the phone call. Just this one call. Everything else could be arranged. She looked at the number, thinking of her mother. *"I'm sorry, Mom, it was the only way I could help you,"* she whispered to herself. She dialed the number.

CHAPTER 12

B renda Jackson had just finished her workout. She left the gym and was heading home. She had thought of Breanne today and it pushed her into a workout frenzy. She missed her little sister and the anger pushed her into a furious workout. She was tired and wanted to go home and rest for a few hours.

She had thought of Allison and where she was and how she was doing. She got home and showered and sat down on the couch with a water and reflected on why today Breanne had been on her mind. It was because Branch, too, had been on her mind. She went back to the episode at Mike Parson's lake house. She knew Breanne was happy with Allison, and it also brought back the thought of Sheila and how she had been attracted to her. She kept losing important people in her life. There was only one left and that one was Allison Branch. The three of them had been close and now the events in their lives had driven them somewhere that left Brenda all alone and miserable.

She opened her trac phone to the only number on it and stared for what seemed like several minutes to her. Brenda just needed to know if she was okay. She needed her friendship and they had always had fun when they had gone out together. It was Branch that helped her with Breanne, keeping her out of trouble and giving Breanne the companion she needed. It was Branch that she looked up to, both her and Breanne did, as the leader. Branch was the one that they all relied on through everything. They had been through a lot together.

Just then, her phone rang. It was a number she did not recognize. She hesitated just a bit as it kept ringing. *Answer it, Brenda.* Finally, she answered, "Hello?"

"Brenda, this is Jake. Something went wrong for Allison. Like I told you before, the doctors could not guarantee anything with the surgery. Today was the first day the bandages came off. It left some scaring, some of it bad. They did their best, but she was hysterical. We had to give her a shot to sedate her."

"Oh, no," Brenda said. "Is there anything I can do to help?"

"No, not right now," Jake said. "I just want to tell you, I think she is going to want to come back to the states and we may need a place to hide for a bit. She's angry, very angry and I don't know if I can control her. The Boss is not happy with her unstable behavior and I have a feeling we may need to run from here," Jake said as he took a deep draw on his cigarette. "I can't talk long but just be thinking of somewhere we can go. I'll let you know when we are on our way. We will all be in danger if we leave. You, me, and Allison. I'll decide by tomorrow."

Jake hung up.

Brenda sat and stared straight ahead.

It was that cocky Parsons and that detective, Marx, that made this happen. It was their fault and they needed to be taken care of, quickly, before it was too late for all of us.

Brenda began to seethe again as the thought of Breanne came rushing back once more. She was beginning to clearly understand Branch's hate for these people. For different reasons, of course, but still she began to feel the pulse that Allison had always felt. It was a dark and ugly pulse that was beginning to beat in her head.

Just then her own phone rang again. Once again, a number she did not recognize. She answered. A voice began to tell her some things she had never known.

"Brenda, you don't know me, but I know Allison Branch. My name is Anastasia and if you use my name, she will know who called you. She has my number. I have something I think Allison and you both would be interested in. It's a letter from Andres and he has left money for Branch and me. I can let you know where you can meet me and you need to let Branch know what I am telling you. You can meet me in Miami, but I want to be sure I hear from Branch first before I tell you where," Anastasia said. "I have the choice to testify in Carrianne's trial, or I can run and choose to help you and Branch. I have chosen to help Branch. Her cut is seventy-five percent of the ten million he has left behind. I get twenty-five percent for handling this transaction. I am the only one who knows where the money is, so don't try to cross me. Branch has my number, so just have her call me and I will let her know where we meet. Once I get my cut, I'm done and I will disappear."

"How do I know this is all on the level?" Brenda asked. "You could be setting us up with the cops. I don't think I buy this story until I talk to Branch."

"Call her, she knows who I am," Anastasia replied. "I have safe places for us to meet. Trust me."

"I really don't trust anyone," Brenda said convincingly.

"I understand, but you had a sister, Breanne, right?" Anastasia asked.

"How did you know that?" Brenda fired back.

"Andres told me everything about the first showdown at Parson's lake house. How Breanne was killed by the cop, how Branch went to jail and how he helped get her out. He told me many secrets. You see, I'm legitimate," Anastasia said with conviction. "You know if I know that, then I know a lot more about all of you."

Brenda paused before responding. *This could still be a set up. But she knows a lot, but so would the cops. You have to call Branch and let her decide. Jake and Allison need to leave there anyway, so it's probably worth the risk if Branch okays the deal.* "Okay, let me call Branch and I can call you back, that is if everything is legit," Brenda said. She hung up...

▲

Jake was pacing. Allison was sleeping after her shot. Jake was really conflicted. He was worried that Allison had become too unhinged for the Boss's liking. He worried that the Boss would eliminate Branch. For that matter, he even worried that the Boss would eliminate him.

As he paced, he looked out the window and he could see for miles. But right here, in front of his face, he couldn't see past his own nose. Things were starting to close in on Jake, and he was starting to panic. He had thought all along that he was rising in the cartel, just like Andres had wanted him too. He had all the help he needed and he didn't lack the smarts, but he did lack the maturity needed to keep things close to the vest. It was starting to work against him. He just couldn't keep from panicking.

Jake started to breathe faster as his own thoughts were beginning to break him down. He heard the phone ring in Allison's room. He rushed in to answer before anyone could hear it.

"Hello, this is Jake, who's this?" he asked.

"It's Brenda," she said slowly. "I need to speak to Allison," Brenda said with a bit of urgency in her voice.

"She's sleeping right now. We had to sedate her after she viewed her face, like I told you. Her surgery didn't work out very well. It left some scaring," Jake said, uncomfortable about giving out too much information.

"Jake, listen, I got a call from this lady Anastasia, and she said she knows Branch, Andres and you. Do you know her?" Brenda asked.

"Yes. What did she tell you?" Jake asked quickly.

"She said she has access to money that Andres left Allison. She wanted to arrange a meeting and let her know where her cut is, and possibly find a way for you both to get to the states and hide out," Brenda said.

"I can't stay on this phone too long, but I will call her myself and make the arrangements. I will call you later when everything is planned. I am not sure what is happening here, but I am feeling we will be needing to run from here. Don't call again. I will call you."

Jake hung up. Outside his door Aberto could hear the conversation. Aberto quietly walked off, he had something to tell the Boss. Jake really liked Aberto, but Aberto didn't like Jake. Not like Garon did. He could use them both to get what he wanted. He could use the step up in the organization and finally, he had found a way. Now to just get the Boss to hear him out...

———▲———

I had to see Joanna. It was nice of Katy to take care of me, but I needed to see Joanna. She couldn't just leave a note and be gone. I got into my car after Katy let me out. I watched her drive away. My mind was in a confused state. The hangover didn't help, but I was so intent on getting Joanna to hear me out and then there was Katy, still there, after all this time, and me still not seeing what she felt for me. I drove towards Joanna's, trying to gather all the strength I needed to convince her she was the one I needed. I felt I was trying to convince myself, too. *Are we best for each other? I had to think it through. We just had to have this conversation. What if she sticks to it? What if she doesn't come back? My life continues to be a long list of what ifs.*

I parked the car in front of her house and went to the door and knocked. I waited a bit and knocked again. Surely, she was in there. No answer. I went and leaned against my car and pulled out my cell phone. I dialed her number. Still no answer. *C'mon, Joanna, answer it. She has to be home. Surely, she's okay?*

Suddenly, a hand touched my shoulder and I spun around quickly. It was Ed Weston, my colleague and friend that introduced Joanna to me.

"She's gone, Mike. She left a few hours ago. She said she had to go back to Pennsylvania to figure some things out. She didn't leave a number. She said she didn't know if she would be back," he said looking down at the ground. He shuffled his feet uncomfortably and asked, "Why don't you come over and have a coffee? You look like you could use one."

"No, no thanks, Ed. I've got plenty to sort out and I just need some time alone," I said shoving my hands in my pockets to get my keys.

"Are you sure?" he asked once more, fixing a hard gaze at me.

"Yes, I'll be fine, Ed," I said as I opened the door of my car to get in. "If you do hear from her…"

"Yeah, Mike, I'll call you," he said finishing my sentence for me.

I got in and pulled out of the driveway, waving to Ed as I put the car in drive. The look on his face was one of concern. Ed had always tried to watch out for me. He rooted for me and my life to improve. The look on his face said it all. He saw me going down the tubes. Maybe I was…

CHAPTER 13

Alberto had some talking to do. He got the Boss to meet him in the outside patio bar. They had a couple of drinks in front of them and he began to get to the point quickly.

"Look, Boss, you may be at the point where you need to do something about the girl. I overheard a conversation Jake had on the phone with some lady. I heard him call her Anastasia. He has plans to leave possibly and I think they're getting money and maybe a place to hide out in the states. If the Feds grab them, they'll turn on you in a hurry. You already have a witness against you in Carrianne. You most certainly don't need another," Aberto said, swirling the whiskey in his glass around the ice.

The Boss seemed pensive about this information. He had worried about Branch since the day she came back from the explosion. She had always had the potential to go off the rails, and the Boss was convinced she would have to be eliminated.

"Thanks for the news, Aberto. You are a good soldier of this organization. Most assuredly, I have figured you and your brother are rising fast in our cartel. There will be top spots for you if we get this thing carried out," the Boss said. "Just follow them closely and watch Jake and Allison for the next two days. I have a few calls to make and I can set something up. I will get back to you shortly with the information you will need," the Boss said, staring out into the dense jungle area where this mansion sat. The Boss took a large drink from his glass of whiskey. "Stephenson will help me set her up. I think he really knows her the best," the Boss said with a smile that Aberto could not read. His smile was steely, sharp, and fixed as if he was holding a secret that no one else knew.

Just a few feet away by an open window, Garon was overhearing the conversation between the Boss and Aberto. He could not believe his ears. He had to tell Jake, they needed to escape. They would certainly kill them if they stayed. Garon liked Jake. They had always gotten along well. But his loyalty to his own brother, against the idea of helping Jake and Branch, now had him conflicted. He had to pick his side carefully and just as Carrianne had been conflicted about loyalty to Jake, Garon was in the same situation.

Garon had to pull Jake aside and let him know, maybe they could get away and he could stay. But he knew that was impossible. His choice was in or out. There wasn't any middle ground. Garon struggled with his decision most of the evening. His brother, Aberto, had talked to him earlier and he didn't bring this up. This concerned Garon, because most times, Aberto had shared everything with him. Not this time. This made Garon uncomfortable and he was now very suspicious that his own brother could turn on him at any minute. This business of drugs and murder had left him mostly void of feelings but he was changing, and he knew his only way out could cost him his life. Once you are in, there is no getting out unless you wanted to risk dying for it. He could not sleep. He was worried he wasn't part of the plan and that they would kill him in his sleep. Paranoid thoughts continued to race through his mind. He needed to get to Jake and Branch and they would all leave together. He texted Jake and told him he was coming to his room. He had something to tell Jake. Garon had made up his mind. He chose his side carefully. He was on Jake and Branch's side. He was going to tell them what was going on and how they could leave together. Now, there was no turning back. At least in the states, Garon had a chance. They all three had to get out.

"*COME ON DOWN*," the text from Jake's phone read.

"*BE RIGHT THERE,*" Garon responded.

He was going now. He slowly walked quietly by his brother's room and slowly walked towards Jake's room. His breathing was shallow and quick as he took a few steps and looked behind him in the dark. He trusted no one. Life was becoming very dangerous for Garon...very dangerous...

▲

I had driven home and settled down on the couch. My life was now back to square one, the same old Mike Parsons that I had always been, unable to change and now almost unwilling to. I needed a drink, but I resisted this one time, for whatever reason, I don't know. I was curious as to how Marx was doing and I felt like calling him. I was thinking how he had gotten me involved in this from the start.

I picked up my phone and called him. He answered on the second ring.

"Hey, Marx. Parsons, here. Just thought you might have something on Branch," I said getting right to the point.

"Not anything, yet. I don't think it will be long though," he said. "Hey, Mike, why don't you come by? We need to go back to the explosion and track this another way. I think they will be back and I wanted to share with you why. If you help me this one last time, then we can end it."

"Yeah, we have lots to talk about. I don't know how I let you talk me into this stuff," I said almost searching for Marx to tell me why. But he was silent.

"Okay, I'll see you in a few minutes," Marx said.

I hung up the phone and it rang immediately. I answered quickly, not looking at the number on my phone, thinking it might be Joanna. It was Margaret.

"Mike, can you please come by, I really need to see you," she sobbed and immediately I knew she was in some sort of distress.

"Margaret, what's wrong?" I asked

"Please come over, there is something I need to show you," she said.

"Okay, look, I have to make a call and then, I will be right there," I said hurriedly.

I hung up and called Marx. I told him I would be about an hour as I had to stop by Margaret's first. I rushed back to my room to get dressed. For some strange reason I had a charge of excitement. For the first time since I started drinking at O'Shea's, I found some sort of purpose to my life. I was back on the case, but first I needed to attend to Margaret.

I jumped in the car and headed to Margaret's to see what she was upset about. It took me just a few minutes to get there. I pulled into the driveway at 6:00 pm. I knocked on her door and she answered. She looked rough and there were tears streaming down her face. Something was terribly wrong here. We went to the living room to sit down, but there were boxes on the couch with papers strewn about. They were papers of Sheila's as I recognized her things, pictures, diplomas, and letters were all over the coffee table.

"I see you've been going through Sheila's things. Do you think that is good for you to do that right now?" I asked.

"Mike, there is something you have to see. I was going through her things, I was still thinking of how I know she couldn't have committed suicide. It just wasn't her, you know that, too," she said trying to hold back more tears. I sat down in the chair next to her and tried to digest this. I wasn't sure that she could have committed suicide either, but her life had taken so many turns it wasn't out of the realm of possibility.

She handed me Sheila's diary. "Mike, please read this. It made me think something horrible," she said.

I began to read the passage and it hit me right in the face. It was dated the night of her death.

"I had a visit from a detective named Allison Branch last night. She said she had some questions about Dad. She said she knew my friends, Brenda and Breanne. She had a lot of questions that made me uncomfortable. She knew personal things about my Dad and she insinuated that he may be having an affair and in money trouble. I asked her to leave and she did after using the bathroom. I am not feeling well and am going to bed now."

"I think she murdered her, Mike. I think Branch killed her," Margaret said.

"But how? I know how you could think that but

how do we know, we have no evidence?" I questioned.

"Look, you know she did the investigation. Why didn't she tell anyone about this entry if she was innocent?" Margaret asked with tears beginning to form again.

"True, but yes...she could have done it...maybe," I said. "Look, Margaret, I'm on my way to see Marx. Maybe he can put some of this together," I said. "Try to put some of this away and I will stop by to see you when I get done at Marx's place."

"Mike, you know Branch killed her. You and I both know it," Margaret said.

Inside, I didn't think she was wrong. I left and got in my car and drove to Marx's place. I had a bad feeling about what Margaret showed me. The diary was on the passenger seat. I grabbed it and took it with me to Marx's door. SHE is a demon. Plain and simple. SHE is a crazy one and somehow, I still feel like someone should have helped that girl a long time ago. But the diary said it. She wasn't innocent in this, I knew it. She had killed my ex-wife. Margaret wasn't wrong, and I hated to leave her there, but I had to show this to Marx. I would return and I told her that I would. I just had to get this to Marx. He would figure out something.

I knocked on the door and Marx answered it almost as fast as my fist hit the door.

"Come in, Mike," he said.

"I have something for you, Marx. Something that hit me right in the face when I talked to Margaret. I brought it with me," I said almost spitting words out of my mouth.

"Come to the kitchen, I am working on a table in

there," Marx said extended his arm to the kitchen area.

We both took a seat at the table, and, not to my surprise, Marx had notes and pictures spread around the table. I could see he had spent some long hours with this. I knew he had some sort of plan in mind.

"Marx, before you start, I have something that Margaret gave me that you have to read. It was the diary that Sheila had written in, and the passage I want to show you is from the night of her death."

He read the passage slowly, intent on every word. He finished and looked up slowly at me, as if he was studying me.

"SHE certainly could have killed her, the diary makes it clear and obviously, as she wasn't feeling well, they could have had a wine or two to drink and then Branch dropped something in Sheila's drink. It's possible. But we're missing some obvious things here that come to light with what you have shown me. There are two people I know about in this investigation that have slid by, Anastasia and Brenda. Somehow, they are in the background. Branch was smart enough to keep them off to the side," Marx explained.

I looked at him quizzically because I had forgotten about this Anastasia person. I remember Marx telling me about her and her involvement with the big man, Andres, but how does she fit with Branch or Brenda Jackson?

"I see how you can think Branch killed her," Marx continued. "That part makes sense. But I think that somehow, Branch and Anastasia had the connection through the big man. This Anastasia was a double dealer and worked for both sides. She could still have a connection and back in Florida is where that could take place. It is just my gut telling me that."

When Marx had a gut feeling, I usually trusted it. Anastasia on both sides? Interesting?

"I just heard from Holmes of the FBI that they are getting closer to the cartel and the Boss. They think they are closing in on them," Andy continued. "I just have the feeling that Branch is going to run with that kid Jake. They're going to make a run for it. The kid is smart but impulsive. She can make him do whatever she wants him to do."

"Geez, we're not going to Florida, are we?" I asked, hoping the answer was no.

"Not yet, but I think some action is going to take place there, but I am not sure when. Trying to guess is difficult. But soon, my friend, soon," he said.

I checked his face and I could see something in him I had not seen in a while. The Andy Marx toughness and determination were coming back. The competitive nature of the number one student in the police academy and the hard, tough intensity that made him the best detective in the department was showing. He looked tired and my first instinct was to run and run fast. But I just had to help, we had become close and I couldn't turn tail and run. Besides, SHE needed to be caught or killed. I couldn't stop now. Like Marx, I was feeling a new addiction, the addiction of trying to find her and end her for good.

"Well, I am in. Count me as one to help. Anything I can do, I am all for it," I said quickly and almost wanting to catch those words and put them back in my mouth, quickly. But it was too late. I was once again in the chase. One way or the other, it was Marx, Branch and me in that eternal triangle that never seemed to end.

"Good," Marx said as he tapped his pen on the table. I have a couple of ideas. We need to find Brenda Jackson though. She is key to finding Branch at the moment. We need to track her down and fast," Marx said.

"Alright, look, I'll give her a call but I need to get back to Margaret. She really needs my help. Call me back around 8:00 tonight. I should be home by then," I said.

"Let Margaret know I am keeping the diary as evidence. It's standard procedure."

"I will. I'll look forward to hearing from you later."

I left Marx's less confused and a bit more focused on Branch than I wanted to be. Danger was much closer than it used to be and once again, I was somewhere in her danger zone, a place I hated and one SHE loved.

CHAPTER 14

Jake was awake in his room, waiting for Garon to come. He was worried about the text. He did not know what was in store but he felt in his bones that something was wrong. He had been a good soldier at all times. It seemed to him now that life in the cartel was becoming extremely dangerous. He was sweating this evening, unable to sleep. He had much on his mind.

He heard the soft knock on his door. He cracked the door and saw Garon's face. He slowly opened the door and let him in. Garon was visibly nervous and he too had sweat on his face as the slow walk to Jake's room had made him nervous.

"Where is she?" he whispered very low.

"She's in her room." Jake said, also in a whisper. He knew something was wrong and that he was about to receive some bad information.

"There's a plot, one to get rid of you and her, maybe me too," Garon said as he continued to keep his voice low. "I'm sure of one thing, we have to move fast. We need to get out of here quickly. We both need to go to her room and let her know, pack just a few things and then we leave early in the morning while they are all still asleep. I know the way out. I really don't know how they are going to get rid of us, but they have something planned and if we wait on them, we will be dead."

"Okay, we all know the tunnel to use, but the alarm has to be disabled first. We both know how to do that," Jake said trying to think fast. "Aberto will be watching us closely so we need to do this in the morning and see if we get out. We need to pack just a few things in the backpack. You have always flown the planes, but that is too risky and they can track us. We can use our fake passports and get to the airport. I can order the tickets on my phone and they can be ready when we get there. I have a connection to a guy at the airport who can get us out quickly. He will gladly take some cash to help us. No luggage and everything is carry on. We'll have to ditch our guns before we get there. When we get to Florida, I have connections to get us new weapons."

"This is risky, but so is staying here. It is time to make a run for it. We don't have time for the perfect plan. But if we wait, we won't make it through the week," Garon said. "If we get out of here, we will make it. Getting out of here without them knowing it is the trick."

"Let me go and talk to her," Jake said. "I'll get her ready to go. She is wounded mentally right now. She is very unhappy with her appearance. It has been a struggle to keep her under control. I'll make sure she is medicated properly, so we'll have to explain things to her before I do that and we will have to keep her close to us on the way out. I'll have the alarm disabled by 3:30 am. We leave at 3:45 am. I have a few calls to make to get us out of the airport in quick fashion. You have to be quiet, Garon. We can't be heard."

"I understand," Garon said.

"Allison already had plans to go to the states, a meeting in Miami, but she doesn't know that the Boss is thinking of eliminating her. It just made our decision to go now a no-brainer," Jake told Garon.

"Look, you know how dangerous this is and without planning, a lot could go wrong," Garon said. "I have made up my mind and it is time to go, but they will come for us. We have to plan to get to them before they get to us."

"It's 12:30, we have little time. Be here by 3:30, and Branch and I will be here together. We leave from here and the alarm will be disabled. Don't be late," Jake said.

Garon just nodded and quietly left Jake's room. Jake waited a few minutes and texted Branch.

"I'M COMING TO YOUR ROOM."

"OKAY, CAN'T SLEEP ANYWAY."

"DONT SAY A WORD, WE NEED TO BE QUIET."

"GOT IT."

Jake wondered to himself if she had already figured this out. She was smart, dangerous, and impulsive. Smart and dangerous were okay, impulsive was not. It was her impulsiveness he had to control for them to reach the states safely. Walking towards her room, he did not know how this would come out. His heart was already beating faster. She was smart and what she may know or have figured out may cause her to act irrationally. Jake must warn her that she had to be under control. This had to be done quietly and swiftly. It was an extremely dangerous move, but so was staying...

_____▲_____

At 3:00 am, I was usually in the middle of terrible dreams, or wide-awake contemplating the rest of my life. Right now, I was thinking of what Margaret told me. *Branch had killed my ex-wife? I couldn't come to grips with that. What if Margaret was wrong? What if that was just not true? But, surely, SHE did it, SHE is evil. Tracking down Brenda Jackson, going to Florida, and the chance of running into Branch, was keeping my mind racing. Since sleep was impossible. I had to get up, I just have to think. Joanna was gone, I just have to accept that and move on. At what point did I no longer care if I lived or died and that this chase with all these crazy people would soon end me? I need some coffee, no, I need a drink, aw hell, I don't know what I need.*

I got out of bed and chose some coffee over a good, stiff scotch. It was probably a good choice at this time of night. While the coffee brewed, I needed to vent, needed someone to talk to. This suspense, this whole list of episodes had basically ruined my life and I wanted to share my ruined life with someone. I thought of Marx but maybe I should let him rest. I thought of Margaret, who probably needed company, too. But she also needed rest. I would just let it go and talk to myself, I suppose. I thought of my brother, James, who he had his own family to deal with. No reason to wake his wife and kids.

I got up and poured myself a coffee. I had just about given up on the thought of sleeping any longer. I was up for the duration of this day probably. One of my bad habits, not sleeping, was going to be the death of me.

I went to the window and peered out into the

darkness. *That was what my life had been. A lot of darkness. I never seemed to find any answers, just lots of questions. What's out there? It's getting late in the happiness business and I am not making it there. I see the lights outside. They give me some hope, but they seem so far away, like they just weren't meant for me, but meant for other people. After all, I just didn't deserve them.*

I looked at one of the larger lights in the distance. It made me think it represented something. Brighter than all the lights around it, this light shone brighter above all the others. Funny, I saw each of the others grow much dimmer as the bright light was dominating. I'm sure it was there every other night, but why am I noticing it tonight? I had looked out of these sliding glass doors on many nights. Why did I not see it before? It made me think of something, it made me think of Katy. She was the bright light, she had always been there. Why had I not seen that?

I picked up my phone and pulled up her contact number. I stared at it for the longest time, my thumb hovering above it for the longest time. I debated with myself, wondering how my fear of ruining one more life would keep me from pressing on her number. But this time, I felt different. Yes, she had always been there, shining bright in the night while I chose the other dull lights. Never being happy. *"Why not Katy?"* Well, why not? She had been there for me always and I repressed what I think I now knew. She was always there to listen, to help, and I had bypassed her every time. I denied that it was her all along. I let her down so much. Somehow, I knew that it was her, but I always tried to keep her from me. *"Call her, press the button, you know it's her, call her!* I looked at the number one last time and looked up at the sliding glass door one last time.

Suddenly, that face that is after me appeared in the glass reflection. *"Do you believe in destiny, Mike? Well, do you?* I jumped and dropped my coffee cup exploding it into pieces on the floor, coffee everywhere. I blinked once, twice, and then it was gone. HER image was no longer there, only the dim lights and the brightest one still there.

I went to the kitchen and got the broom and some towels. I cleaned up my mess and sat back on the couch. I never made the call to Katy. Geez, my world is so crazy. All because of HER...

CHAPTER 15

They walked slowly and without a sound but their breathing. They had almost reached the door of the tunnel that would lead them out. A door would be waiting. Opening it quietly was a must. They had only small backpacks with essential items if they had to run. Garon reached the door first and carefully unlocked the steel door. He had done so with no noise, and they quietly slipped into the tunnel. Garon turned to lock the door from the inside and they began to make their way. They used their flashlights and made it to the first turn. There would be five more turns to make before they could get to the outside door.

They had made it to turn number five and the panel with the alarm was in front of Garon. He shone his flashlight on the panel and pushed the correct button. This would be his last act inside the cartel mansion. He soon would be all in with Jake and Branch, and they would no longer work for the Boss. They were on their way to the jeep that would take them through the jungle trail and to the road that would lead them to the city.

They closed the door behind them and were now in a completely different world. They were now no longer working for the cartel and running was just as dangerous, if not more, than running from the law. They got in the jeep and Garon started it up. He drove through the dense jungle with no lights for the first one hundred yards. He flipped on the lights and they were gone. They were really leaving the cartel. Garon and Jake were sweating profusely, but not Branch. She seemed to Garon to be oblivious to the danger they had taken on. It was because she was deep in thought.

Soon, I will be back in Florida. I have to meet with Brenda and Anastasia. There is something for me. Money. Money that had been left to me by Andres Montoya. Yes, that had to be done first. Then I could hunt him down. Yes, that Mike Parsons was going to die. He was going to die by my hand. So would Marx and that stupid bartender, Katy. It would be easy to get them all in the same place. I would get them to a place that would be the perfect ending point. It would be a scene that I could totally control. I had planned this for so long during my recovery. They won't have a chance this time. It was my best plan, the best ever. There would be no escaping this time...

"Allison, hey, Allison!" Jake poked her and brought her out of her semi-trance.

"Yeah, I'm okay, Jake. I'm okay," she replied with a silly smile on her face that Jake had seen before.

"Where are we?" she asked.

"In Rio," Garon said as he drove, "and I think we are being followed."

"Damn!" Jake exclaimed. "It just can't be them. We

were quiet, made no noise at all."

"I'll make a few turns to lose them. We're so close to the airport, but we have to get out and go on foot, if we can. I know a back way through some alleys that will get us to a place to ditch the car. Stay close and remember to ditch the guns before we get to the airport parking lot. We can't take them with us," Garon said trying to remain cool as he drove recklessly through the back streets and alleys of the city. "I have a contact to call and he can take us the rest of the way to Aeroporto Internacional of Rio. There I have arranged a helper to get us boarding passes."

They had made it to a nearby highway, and it was time to get out and walk. Garon got on the phone and called his contact, who would be there soon. They had lost their follower, but he couldn't be too far behind. They hid in the ditch and waited as Garon talked to his contact on the phone. He was three minutes away. *Almost there, almost there, he thought to himself.* He could hear each person breathe short, quick breaths. One more minute to go.

"Let's go, he's almost here," Garon said and all three stood up and got into the car that pulled off onto the shoulder. They had escaped their follower. The contact delivered them to the airport...

--- ▲ ---

The Chemist had a job to do, not for the Boss, but for himself. He had waited many years for this one. In a strange way, he enjoyed what he did. His plans and engineering of explosions were something he changed each time. Each job was different and each victim should have a different scenario. He had been almost perfect in their executions. He had missed once, and he would make up for that one. But for now, he had a unique job. This one was all on his own, a debt from his past that needed to be paid.

He made his way to the house of his old army sergeant, who had a beautiful home in Florida, retired now for the past two years. He left his car and now walked down his street dressed all in black to not be seen. When he got there, he saw the sergeant's car was parked in the driveway and it was dark, very dark on this cloudy night, one he had picked with great care. He did his work swiftly and carefully and then moved to the end of the driveway. He quickly blew a kiss towards the house and left hurriedly back up the street to his car. No one had seen him, he was sure. He knew how to hide himself. He would come back in the morning at dawn and watch from afar. This was his best job yet and his most satisfying.

At dawn, he returned and from a distance stayed in his car and used the binoculars. He kept an eye on the house. The sergeant appeared and was walking down the drive, waving goodbye to his wife. He got into the car and turned the key. The flames and smoke leapt high into the air, and the firetrucks would soon be here.

Mission Accomplished! He drove away, never going near the scene, happy and content and above all else, with no regrets.

Garon, Jake, and Allison were making their way to their gate to board their flight. They had already gotten their boarding passes from Garon's contact. Disguised and patient, they tried not walk fast. They didn't want to be noticed. Jake was worried because he knew who was following and if Aberto caught them, it would be over. Jake looked over at Allison, and she had the walk of a person in control, confident, and poised. Her hoody pulled over her head mostly hid her face that had changed dramatically. He wanted to help her get her damaged face repaired, but right now, getting to the states meant everything. Fake passports and fake ID's had helped them pass all the checkpoints, and they were almost there. The gate, number ten, was coming into view.

Garon sped up a bit, and Jake and Allison increased their stride. They had made it and their wait was ten minutes. It would be the longest ten minutes of their life, but once on board they would feel better. They sat separately at the gate and would sit separately on the plane. It would help in case someone identified one of them and not to put them together. They suspiciously looked around at their fellow passengers, but more importantly, they looked often down the hall they had come from. Someone had trailed them and if they would get caught, it would more than likely be now.

Jake looked at the clock. Boarding time just three minutes away. They had to make it. They were so close.

The speaker blared out, "Flight 302, headed for Miami, Florida, is now boarding at gate 10."

They lined up and Garon kept looking behind him for their follower. He knew he would recognize him if he saw him at all. He kept looking for his brother, Aberto, who he was leaving for good. If anyone would spoil this plan, it was Aberto. But he never did show. They boarded the plane, and they would not speak to each other until they got back inside the next airport.

It was a short time for the taxi along the runway. The plane picked up speed and was nearing take off. The big bird lifted off the ground and they began their assent. Jake felt better, but not Garon. Garon somehow knew someone would be on their tail in the states. He just knew it...

Back in the Rio Aeroporto Internacional, Aberto had found Garon's contact. He had gotten all the information he needed from him. The contact was found an hour later, in a restroom stall, throat cut and dead as a door nail. Aberto was on a plane headed to Miami and confident he would find them. He would get rid of all three of them, just as the Boss had told him. He had to, his brother had betrayed him and the Boss. The thought that Garon could betray his own brother and the Boss caused Aberto to fume. The anger inside him was mounting, but he needed to stay calm. He needed a plan to find them and he would. He had to, or else the Boss would make sure he was never heard from again. *Be calm. Be calm and make your plan. You know his contacts and you know the neighborhoods. Just think and be organized. That Garon! How could he do this? He will pay and that crazy girl and Jake, I'll get rid of them, too. But that girl, she worries me. There's just something about her. Something tells me that I shouldn't sell her short. The other two, Garon and Jake, it's playing the chess game. I know that game. But with her, it was a mind game and she has a way of seducing you into playing. I don't know that game as well.*

Aberto pulled out his phone and started to make notes. He was, by nature, a careful, thinking man. He sped his thumbs across his cell furiously. His plan would come together. He stopped for a minute and thought, *but that woman, that crazy woman. You need to prepare for her. Your plan must have a way to protect yourself from her. SHE can't be trusted. SHE's evil.* He went back to his plan...

CHAPTER 16

I called two more times. Joanna never answered. I was not feeling like work today. I could feel Joanna slipping away with each passing day. I knew that note she left would be the last thing that would ring over and over in my mind. She was gone for good and I was having trouble coming to grips with it.

I thought I was having the best relationship of my life and now, I was back to the old me. I had come back to where Mike Parsons always seemed to be. I had seen a therapist, read all the motivational quotes, and self-talked in a positive way. Yet, here I was, coming full circle back to the same valley I always seemed to find myself. Depressed, self-loathing, and tired, I shuffled off to the shower. My feet felt like lead and I just had to get with it. I trudged on, but only made it to the bed.

Stop it! You're acting like a little kid. You're a grown-up man and you have to fight. Get yourself off this bed and get with it. Face the facts. Sheila's dead, Margaret's going downhill, Joanna is gone. You have very few people to count on Marx, James and then there's Katy...yes, once again, there was a constant. It was Katy. Hasn't it always been Katy? Always ready to help you, always ready to fill in the blanks, yet you never let her in. Like you're some big brother protecting her and she now stands taller than you. You haven't changed, Mike. She has. She's stronger and adjusting to her life. You're the one who is collapsing like a folding chair. Yes, Katy is stronger and you are the one going downhill...

Just then, I heard my cell ring and it was Marx.

"Hello," I said glumly into my phone.

"Hey Mike, this is Marx. You sound like you lost your best friend."

"Actually, I think I did," I said looking down at my feet.

"What do you mean?" he asked.

"Well, I never thought the need to share it with you the day I brought you the diary, but Joanna left me. It's the reason I'm down in the dumps," I said.

Marx was quiet, and he let it sink in. "Hey, I'm sorry, man. I hate to hear that for you." It was his best attempt at being sympathetic. Something he never seemed to get a handle on.

"Thanks, but it has put me in a bad place. I feel like I'm slowly slipping into something I may not get out of. I have to do something, you know, to get my mind off of it."

"Well, I think I have something for us to do," Marx replied. "I got a call from the FBI. With the information they got from Carrianne, they finally raided the mansion and found no one there. Looks like the cartel has slipped them. The FBI feels like they don't know where they are headed but my guess is Florida. We'll just sit tight and see what happens."

"Well, if you need me to go, I will."

▲

I felt more alone than I ever had at this point. Leaving in the morning and needing to pack, I started to get up but instead, picked up my cell and looked up Katy's number. I stared at it for quite a while. *Should I? I've put decisions on hold like this all the time. Self-debate always made me slow to do what I should. I ask myself way too many questions. Go ahead, call her.*

Finally, I pushed her contact number and the phone rang, one ring, two rings, three and then "Hi, this is Katy. I can't come to the phone right now, but if you leave a message, I will call you back...beep." There it was, the dreaded message that pops up when someone is busy or maybe even doesn't want to talk to you.

"Katy, this is Mike. I just wanted to check on you and see if you were okay, give me a call if you want, I'd like to talk with you sometime soon. See ya later."

Florida again, back to the scene of my last nightmare. I pictured it all again, there I was running down the street. They were chasing me and closing fast. I was closing in on the intersection and then I crossed it. Boom! That explosion, knocking me to the ground, shaking my whole body, was loud and the flash of light was blinding. Then I saw HER, hair smoldering, holding her face, staggering into a car. It sped away and then Marx grabbed me and got me to a sitting position. He called for help to assist me and then he was gone. Speeding off after HER. He never found her. Where is she? When will I see her again? In Florida or back here in Milwaukee? Maybe we will meet in some venue I have never seen before. I don't know, but if I do ever see HER again, could I do it, could I pull that trigger?...

Just then I heard my cell ring.

"Hello, Katy. Glad you could call back," I said.

"Hi, Mike, what's going on?" she asked.

"Can you come by? I have a couple of things I want to talk with you about. I can explain it when you get here, I just don't want to do it on the phone," I said.

"Sure, I can. I just got off work so let me go home and clean up and I'll be there in an hour," she replied.

That voice, that sweet, charming voice. What a soothing effect it had on me!

"See you soon," I said and hung up.

Katy sped up as she left the parking lot. She had not heard from Mike since she took him in after his rousing, drunk evening. She was sure it would be longer and really wasn't ready for this call. Going home to clean up and "freshen up" would give her time to compose herself.

Why does this man do this to me? How does he do that? I hear his voice and it sends a chill up my back. I see him and I blush in the face. No one has ever done that to me. But he let me down. I can't count the number of times he did. Face it, Katy, you always wanted him. You still do. But be strong. Being weak got you nowhere and he needs strong. He needs ME strong. He needs ME.

Katy pulled into the driveway and almost ran inside. She took a quick shower and dressed quickly in casual wear, but not too casual. Her appearance had a purpose. Katy knew how to dress. She understood the nuances of looking good. Sometimes, it just came naturally to her. She quickly finished and locked everything up and headed to her car. She was excited to be going to see him, but she wanted to temper that excitement and be rational. She didn't want to be hurt again.

I showered and dressed in jeans and an untucked shirt. It seemed like a long time since I saw Katy and, at least this time, I would see her with clear and sober eyes. The last time I saw her, when she was nursing my hang over, there was a more confident, stronger Katy. She was more mature than I remember her being. She didn't look like my "bartender friend" anymore. Yes, there was something quite different about her.

The knock on my door told me Katy was here. I went to the door and opened it. At first, I stood there, almost stunned but them caught myself and found the words. She looked beautiful. After all these years, she's just not a cute kid any more. She was totally stunning.

"Katy, uh, come in, please," I stammered.

"Thanks, Mike. I was glad to hear from you," she said slipping off her light jacket.

"Please, come in and sit down. There is a lot I want to tell you," I said. "Hey, do you want a drink?"

"Sure, do you have any wine?" she asked.

"Yes, just one last bottle. It has your name on it," I said and went to the kitchen to get the corkscrew.

I opened the bottle and poured her a glass. I made myself a scotch on the rocks and then brought both drinks to the living room.

"You look great, Katy."

"Thanks, you look quite handsome yourself."

"Well, thanks, but I don't always feel that way lately."

"Have you heard from Joanna?" she asked, wanting to get that question solved first.

"No, I tried to call, but no answer. I think she's gone for good. But, let's talk about some other things.

There are some other things I need to tell you."

"Oh?" as her brows raised a bit.

"Yes, Marx and I might be going to Florida. He has a lead on HER and he wants me to go back with him," I said.

"That's crazy, isn't it?" she asked taking a long sip of her wine.

"Well, yes and no. It's crazy because we could run into Branch again. But not so crazy because I think Marx knows the people she is connected to there, and we are the hunters this time, not the hunted."

"Mike, I don't know, Allison is sneaky, downright evil. Are you sure it's not a set up?" Katy asked.

"Well, I guess that's a possibility, but I trust Marx and his instincts," I said. "I think he knows her better that even I do."

I took a sip of the scotch and looked at Katy. Something was going through her head. I felt she didn't want to look me in the eye. But finally, she did, and said, "Mike, this thing really scares me. I mean you and Marx going off on some kind of manhunt. You keep picking at this sore and it's going to bleed. She's evil and you know it. You know, I can't just let you go there. I could lose you."

There, she said it. What she intended **not** to say. She had been the passive one, the one who always held on to hope that someday, someway, Mike Parsons would love her. It was hide and seek, little playful kid games, but not anymore. Katy wanted Mike to know, right now, that she had always loved him. She was getting wiser about knowing herself and what she wanted. She was being direct. Finally.

I put my drink down and reached for her hand, it was warm in mine, rubbing the back of her hand, I looked at her like I never looked at Katy before. The touch of her hand, so smooth and delicate, made me feel better than any other human touch I had felt before. We had known each other for so long, but this time, yes, it was electric. These five to ten seconds put life into me. I know that seems like a short time, but it was doing just that, putting a charge back into my soul. A simple thing, not complicated and not lasting long.

"You won't lose me, Katy," I said, "you won't."

"Mike, can you sit by me?" she asked.

I sat my scotch down and moved over and sat down beside her. I knew she needed to he held. I put my arm around her and gently pulled her closer to me. She rested her head on my shoulder and after a few seconds, she looked up at me.

"Mike, I'm worried. Worried that if you go, you won't come back. That I'll never see you again."

"I might have to go. This will never end if I don't confront HER. I can't run from HER forever."

"How ironic," she said. "Ironic in the fact that I had run from you so long, when I really felt like running to you the whole time. You wouldn't let me in, you kept me at a distance. I never gave up on you. I had always hoped that someday, some way, we would be together. I see what you are saying, but I want you to know, right now, I am running to you and I don't want you to run away from me."

"Sometimes the thing you are always trying to keep from happening happens," I said pulling her yet closer to me, our eyes locking and searching for what was on the inside, searching for truth.

I kissed her. I kissed her long and passionately. I felt her soul. The feeling gave me great hope, that for some reason, I felt the right thing with Katy. That right thing was knowing that her person, her heart, and her soul should be handled carefully. *No more games here. Be careful with Katy. Be careful with her heart, her mind and her soul. For her sake and mine, neither one of us could afford another speed bump in the relationship road. We didn't have another comeback left...*

CHAPTER 17

We got no further than that kiss, but I felt good about Katy. We are still not in that relationship, the one that is commitment. Neither one of us is sure of ourselves, but are just enjoying each other's company. Marx was on his way to pick me up and how Katy looked was still fresh in my mind. I felt that things had come full circle for me in some ways. I felt as though Katy had always been there and I always felt something for her. I couldn't bring myself ever to admit it. I wasn't sure, and I don't think she was either, but for now, this new mystery of what Katy and I are, it's intriguing.

———▲———

Aberto knew the Boss was upset. He could tell by the sound of his voice and after landing at the airport, Aberto was desperate again to pick up their trail.

"You better not lose them," he said sternly into the

phone. "I want them both dead."

"Look, Boss, I will find them, don't worry. I will make the plans to take care of them. I know who to call," Aberto said, not knowing if he could come through on that promise or not. They could disappear without a trace and he knew that Garon knew how to protect them. He had to think like Garon or he would become just another dead body in a long line.

"I can't believe you let them get away," the Boss responded. "I'm sending Stephenson back to the states. Wait for him. He knows a lot and will have the right connections if you end up back in her home territory. It's a risk, but I have to do this. Stephenson owes me and I know he can help you. Find them, track them, and he will call you. Let him know where you are staying and he will meet you there. Protect him, as he is a suspect in a cold case there, and he will have to be disguised. His picture has been all over American television for years now."

"Don't worry, Boss. No way I will let them get away," Aberto responded.

"They better not..." Click. The Boss hung up.

Better not or what? I'll tell you what. I'm dead, that's what. I'll find those traitors and they will be finished. It has to be that way or I am finished.

Aberto dialed his phone and made a call while he was walking towards ground transportation. The voice on the other line answered.

"Yes."

"Aberto here. I've lost the prey, but I will find them soon. I will need your help. Wait, let me call you right back," Aberto said and hung up.

He couldn't believe it. He spotted them at a taxi, getting ready to get in. He couldn't believe his good luck. Aberto jumped into a taxi parked a few cars down from them. He told his driver to follow the cab ahead when they pull out. He waited.

"There, there they go. Follow that cab," Aberto said.

Aberto pulled out his cell and texted to his contact.

"CAN'T BELIEVE I FOUND THEM. IN A CAB AHEAD. WILL CALL YOU WHEN I GET TO THE DESTINATION."

"GOT IT" the contact responded in text.

Aberto put his phone back in his pocket and smiled. He had three things to do. One, after Stephenson arrived in the states, he had to make contact with him. Two, he had to make sure his contact was available to help with his plan. And the third thing, well, that's the one that made him smile the most...

Katy woke up in her empty bed still thinking about her time with Mike last night. Although she had no intention of caving in, she couldn't stop the thoughts that were running through her mind. She wanted to be careful and she didn't want to be hurt, but she felt that this time, maybe it was there for them. She didn't want to have false hope and be let down again. No matter how hard she tried to remain calm, there was this thing she had for Mike, and it wasn't going away.

*I've tried to stay away and tried to put him out of my mind. Even when I had him brought to my house to sober up, I thought I had gotten over him. I was strong then and played that part well. But it was just acting. You have never gotten over that man, just admit to that fact. Our kiss last night was real. I felt it, didn't I? It went all the way to my toes. All the time he has tried to **not** love me, on the inside, I think that he always has. And me, I never stopped loving that man. You know, Katy, I don't think you can love* *anyone else.*

Katy ended her self-talk and went on to the kitchen for coffee. Two more weeks of class and she would be ready to get a new job. Nick had been great, but art was her love and the thought of being in the field of graphic design appealed to her. Soon she would be out of the bar business and into a steady job where she didn't have to deal with the late nights. She was looking forward to it.

Her thoughts went back to Mike. Katy always worried a lot and Mike's potential trip to Florida was increasing her worry. *I saw HER, I know HER and what SHE can do. But she may have changed again and I won't know, I won't know when or where she could strike again. I was captive, not once, but twice! I know what SHE is capable of doing. And the hate, the hate in those crazy eyes...*

Katy opened her eyes and told herself to get ready for class. She showered and dressed and got her jacket. She turned off the lights. She thought about the kiss last night once more. It made her smile and she was going to be alright today. *There was a chance, wasn't there? Yes, Katy, yes, there is a chance.* She set her alarm and left the house.

CHAPTER 18

J ake, Allison, and Garon had arrived at the exact place where a room had already been rented for them by an American contact that had been cultivated by Garon during the time of his many visits to Miami. His contact, one Anastasia, had made the arrangements but would not be staying there with them. Garon was to call when they had arrived.

Garon picked up the key in the lobby and moved quickly with his fellow travelers and went immediately to their room. He made a quick call to Anastasia to let them know they had arrived. He gave her instructions to call when she had a meeting place for them to meet with her.

"Look, Anastasia, I think the Boss has put the trail on us. If my thinking is right, it would be Aberto. Any arrangements you make will have to be made with care," he said quietly.

"I am sending a man to meet you with the guns and ammo that you need," she said. "We will have to meet quickly as you won't be able to stay in one place too long. Make sure you are disguised and meet your contact in the parking garage that is two blocks west. You know him as you have worked with him before. Eight this evening on the second floor and he will only be there ten minutes, so, don't be late. He will be in the white delivery van with bread company logo."

"I will be wearing a work shirt, glasses, ballcap, and fake beard. There was not much I could bring, but we each have some disguises in our backpack. I will get in touch with you later when I return about when and where we can meet," Garon said, starting to hurry as he really didn't how much time they had. Everything was a great risk. He hung up and explained the plan to Jake.

Allison had gone to the bathroom and was looking at her face in the mirror. As much as the doctors did their best, her face was scarred and there was no doubt that she was no longer the stunning beauty she had been. She took her meds out and popped one in her mouth and took a drink of water. *I see a little Lynette, a little Allison, and a lot of a stranger I don't know. Look at you, you are hideous! You will get them you know. Your plan is the best. But it is the last time, the final time. I will put them all in their graves. Marx, Katy, and especially you, Mike. Yes, YOU! It will be over soon and there is no way you can get out of this one. You'll come right to me. Go ahead, try and be the hero. You won't have a chance. Just me and you, face to face. Yes, just me and you...me and you...*

"Allison, honey," Jake whispered, carefully placing his hands on hers that had a white-knuckle grip on the sink. "It's okay, easy now, easy."

Her grip slowly loosened on the sink. She turned to face Jake and he held her by the shoulders with both hands as he tried to console her.

"I'm ugly, Jake, aren't I?"

"No, you were never ugly. You're beautiful and you always have been," lying to calm her but knowing he had to help get this fixed. He really didn't need her going off the rails. Everything they did now was dangerous and if she couldn't hold it together, they would never survive. "Look, why don't you take one more pill and lie down for just an hour. Things are going to be okay, I promise."

Allison dropped her head, somehow knowing Jake was only trying to make her feel good. She didn't have much left in her life to depend on except Jake, Garon, and Brenda. She was starting to feel desperate and she wanted to scream, but Jake had convinced her to take another pill. She laid down and soon she was asleep on the bed.

▲

I went to Marx's around eleven. Andy was looking tired, and I studied him for just a few moments. He had such a neat and clean demeanor and mine, well, kind of messy and ugly. I was thinking back to the time when he came to my apartment with Branch. Clean cut, no facial hair, and smartass Andy was how I looked at him back then. Now I was seeing aging Andy Marx, a man who had been through a lot, and it was starting to show.

Marx had brought his briefcase with all the notes about these cases. I had a feeling we weren't going out for beers but would be stuck in here for hours reviewing the notes.

I was right as Marx began to spread the pictures, notes, and information he had about the case on the table. Ever since Branch escaped him last time, Marx had become more obsessed with her. He was going to find her somehow and when he found her, he was taking no prisoners. I didn't even have to ask, I just knew. We both pulled up chairs close to the information and began to study. We looked over pictures and documents, picking them up and then putting them back in place. Marx picked up the picture of the Big Guy, one Andres Montoya, and studied it for a long time.

"This guy," he said, "this guy has something more to do with this, even in death. Somehow his story isn't over."

"What could that possibly be?" I asked.

"Money," he replied. "He had to have money as he had quite a large drug operation going. Where is that money?"

"It could be anywhere, I suppose," I said stating the obvious.

"But think a second, Carrianne Martinez, during her testimony, revealed that Andres was her real father. If that is the case, he probably left Jake and her some money somewhere and it could be in a million places," Marx said.

"What about the farm?" I asked. "If he could bury bodies at the farm, why wouldn't he keep the money there?"

"Too obvious to hide it there," Marx replied. "But wait, remember that guy that came by your car in that truck and rapped on your window. The tobacco-spitter is what you called him. Do you remember that guy?"

"Yes," I replied, "he had a dark complexion, not real tall, and heavy stubble. But, didn't your guys check him out?"

"They were supposed to, but we got the call to get to Florida as the FBI had a bead on Branch. They never did go out there," Marx said.

He quickly picked up his phone and dialed the office.

"Hey, Jim. Marx here. I need you to check out a guy who lives out by the Montoya farm. Do some research and see what you come up with. Get back to me as soon as you can." Marx hung up and looked up at me. "Think of all you can, Mike, about that guy. He could be our only connection back to Branch."

CHAPTER 19

The Chemist had been in France when he got the call. He never had been caught or even a suspect in the explosion that had killed his old Army sergeant. He had made his way easily to France. He had the best connections, the best disguises, and also the best mind. He had always known how to plan, to arrange, and especially he knew how to hurt others without a conscious. Once in fourth grade, he took a pair of scissors and raised them to stab another student. The teacher quickly caught him and stopped him. He was furious as the teacher took him to the principal. He was suspended from school and referred for mental evaluation. His wealthy parents went through the motions, maintaining that their boy was just fine after he had spent the minimum sessions in therapy that was recommended. Besides, it was the other boy's fault for teasing him.

After that incident, Jeremy Todd, aka The Chemist, would go through many like experiences in junior high and high school in South Philadelphia, Pennsylvania. He fought often and was suspended from school sometimes more often than he attended. He did find one teacher he could relate to. His teacher in electronics and technology at Vocational Tech School his junior year took an interest in him. For two years, he learned much in class and even on the internet as his thirst for the subject grew. He did all the projects to perfection. His mind just worked that way. He made A's consistently in this class. The only A's he ever received.

By the end of his senior year, his teacher, an ex-army specialist talked to him about enlisting and that he had a special talent that could be used in the military. Jeremy liked the idea and enlisted right out of high school. He would also become an E-4 Specialist, trained specifically in explosives. He knew his business so well, he was given the tough assignments that required destruction of sites, weapons, and sometimes even people. He was in charge of his small group of men. He was the best and they all knew it and all the destruction he initiated, he did so without a conscious.

After his hitch was up, he could never find a job that interested him like he had in the military. He began to feel aimless and then found work making more money than he ever had running some drugs back in Philly. He had a lot of cash and nice cars. He claimed to others that he had rich parents and was just an entitled kid. Most believed him. His Boss, The Boss of one of the largest drug cartels in South America, saw him as productive. Even so, when the Boss learned from Garon about Jeremy and his explosives experience in the military, the Boss had other plans for him and he had Garon bring him to Brazil. Jeremy was about to be made an offer he could not resist. The money was crazy good and he would get to do what he always liked, destroying things.

He had made up his mind a long time ago that he would get the most satisfaction from destroying anything and everything he could. He had no conscious.

He settled back in his seat on the plane and fastened his seat belt as they were about to land in Florida, USA. Arrangements had already been made by Aberto to have transportation from the airport. He was told by Aberto to look for the cab with the red card taped to the windshield. The wheels hit the ground and Jeremy Todd repeated in his mind, "cab with the red card, cab with the red card." Jeremy's mind was now at work, already contemplating his next job. Damn, he loved his job...

▲

The tobacco-spitter was nowhere to be found. The police had sent a car out there with the number two in charge under Andy Marx, Jim Schaffer. Jim knew who he was looking for by description only. The old Middleton farm was deserted when they got there. His men went up and down the road seeking information from neighbors. The neighbors could only tell them they knew of no one that fit the description of the tobacco spitter.

Jim drew the conclusion that he must have been Andres Montoya's hired hand and had flown the coop. It was a dead end, and he was sorry to tell Andy he had come up with nothing. Jim and his men had spent the better part of the day investigating.

The tobacco spitter was dangerous indeed. He was holed up in a motel and waiting for a phone call from Anastasia. His cut of the money Andres had left was small, but large enough to make his task worth the effort. He had worked for Andres for years, in the streets, as well as, on the farm. He was fairly inconspicuous and hardly left the farm. But the last incident had flushed him to other parts of the state.

He had been in Florida when the cartel held Mike Parsons and his friends. He had been one of the armed guards that Carrianne Martinez had fooled when they escaped. He had always had the idea that he should have shot them all, but Andres had let that woman play her games. Now he had been on the run and waiting for the time to hand over the money, the money Andres had trusted him to take care of, minus his part, of course.

That night, his police sketch appeared on the news. It was time to head somewhere more populated. He was heading somewhere, not in his old truck, but his brand, new Jaguar, compliments of doing work for the Boss and the cartel. It was work that had slowed somewhat since the incident and it was time to blend into a big city, it was time to run again. The heat was on and he was feeling it. With his delivery of the money, he would get another cut soon, he was running out of money, and he needed the cash to survive until he could get back to the streets. He called the Boss to let him know he was on the run and where he was going. The Boss had told him they were flushed out of Brazil by the FBI because of what Carrianne had told them. He hung up and called Anastasia. He told her that the cops had posted his picture and if they wanted the cash, they needed to meet up soon. They didn't have much time left.

William Montaldo looked at his image in the mirror. His stubble had now grown to a full beard. He put on a pair of fake glasses and he was now, in his mind, unlike the sketch on television. He packed the rest of his things and headed out of the motel and to his new Jag and threw the bag of cash in the trunk. He would always let the Boss know where he was located. You don't cross the Boss. Not like Carrianne, Garon, and Jake. They would get what they deserved, but William would play it straight.

He started the car. What a smooth machine it was. William Montaldo, the tobacco spitter, was heading for Chicago.

CHAPTER 20

Garon was disguised and walking to the parking garage. He was only thinking of survival and was alert to all things around him. He knew Aberto was lurking nearby and maybe even watching him now. He had to zig zag his way to the parking garage. The quicker he could get to the bread truck and get to his room, the better.

He headed into the parking garage and made his way swiftly to the second floor for his meeting with his contact. He saw the van sitting all by itself, parked near the east end of the floor. He walked quickly but, yet cautiously, as he kept alert for any signs of a set-up. As he approached, the door to the bread truck opened and his contact stepped out with a carry bag loaded with the supplies and guns they needed. They did not speak but Garon took the bag from the man. The man nodded and got back in the truck, started it, and sped away. All alone, Garon made his way back to the steps to take him back to the first floor and out of the garage.

He mostly held his breath and was sweating from the Florida humidity. He reached the last step and he heard a car racing along the first-floor concrete. He took two steps back up into the stairwell and watched as the car flew out of the garage. *Probably some kid trying to peel out, but be careful, make sure the car clears the garage and moves on.*

Garon stepped out of the stairwell making sure he did not see that car again. Exhaling, he felt safe enough to leave the garage. He pulled out his cell and told Jake to meet him at the back entrance and let him in. He then walked on towards the hotel. His sunglasses made everything look darker than it really was and he began to walk faster as his instincts told him to do just that. *Jake better be there. I don't want to be waiting outside. They could be anywhere. They could be following me right now. Calm down and don't walk too fast.* Garon was sweating even more as he reached the hotel parking lot. He was about ten feet from the door. He reached back to make sure he had his weapon accessible in his waistband, just in case something went wrong.

Garon knocked on the door twice and reached back to grab his weapon, hoping Jake was on the other side to open it. The door came open and he saw that it was Jake and he was safe. They quickly moved together to the room and went inside. Allison was still asleep and Jake was not sure about leaving her alone in the room. But she did wake up when Garon and Jake came inside.

"What's going on?" she asked sleepily as they both stood next to her bed.

"I just picked up the guns and ammunition that we need to survive," Garon said. "We are going to need a path out of Florida soon. What about that meeting with Anastasia?" he asked.

Allison had sat up in bed and was more alert than she had been. "I can call her now, we have to do that meeting tomorrow. It will be me, Jake, and you, Garon, meeting with her."

Allison picked up her phone and very shortly it rang before she could dial. The voice on the other end was Anastasia.

"Allison, our contact called, just now. He wants us to meet up with him soon. Seems like his picture is out in the news and he wants to get this done quickly and disappear. I want to make sure everyone is on the same page before we head to meet him," Anastasia said. "He is keeping me posted on his location. He will only tell me and he wants no trouble, just to get his cut and run."

"Alright, look," Allison started. "let's meet at *The Deuce* at about 7 tomorrow. We can blend in pretty well there. Don't be late. We need to do this quickly and then leave in the night. Jake can arrange for a car to use and then we can all leave together. It should just be the four of us, Jake, me, you, and Garon. Then, we head on to meet the contact. See you at 7."

Allison looked up at Jake and Garon. They seemed to understand the conversation. Jake had a look of concern on his face.

"I wish we could just take off," Jake said rubbing his chin. "Seems like too many people involved and it's hard for me to trust too many people here. I know the contact. He worked out at Andres' farm in Wisconsin. His name is William Montaldo. I know William, I trust him. He was loyal to Andres. I just hope he understands that the Boss will get to him, too, if he doesn't disappear soon. That's why we have to move quickly. We have to trust each other. That means all of us including Anastasia and William."

"Brenda, too," Allison chimed in. "Don't forget, Brenda is involved, too. There are five of us and we have to protect each other. It is dangerous and if one person breaks, we could all go down," Allison said, beginning to feel like her old self, like a leader. She felt she was in charge now, not Garon, not Jake, no one else. It was her game now and those eyes were starting to come to life. She had the connection to all of them and most importantly, her connection to Andres trumped everyone else's. *Everyone else's except Jake. Jake was the impulsive son that Andres kept secret for years. Would she be able to trust him? She had so far, but she had him mesmerized.*

"Right," Jake answered with more confidence now as he now felt more emboldened by his heroine, Allison Branch. "We all have to stick together. Have a plan and stick to that plan. We'll meet tomorrow and then head to our contact when Anastasia lets us know where he is located. Then we take the money and disappear for good."

Garon looked back and forth from Jake to Allison. Garon was just trying to stay alive and not be killed by the Boss. But where did he fit into their plans? There was no money in it for him. Surely, they would give him a cut. He had the connections that had gotten them here and he had risked his life to help them escape. He had made his decision to split with the boss and Aberto. That was done and there was no turning back.

"Alright, listen, I will get a car us to pick us up at 6:30 and we will be at *The Deuce* at 7:00 straight up. We get the meeting done and then head out when we find out the location of William Montaldo. We can't stick around long," Garon said. "We take our things with us. We don't want to leave clues behind."

Garon made the call and arranged for the car. They now had just a few hours to get ready and they would be out of Florida soon. *The sooner the better*, Garon was thinking. *They have to be close. Aberto is smart and he knows me, he knows where we might be. They could be watching us right now. Every move is dangerous.*

They would all three get ready to go. There was a plan, they just had to stick to it. Garon had been their best bet for survival and, so far, he had come through. So far....

CHAPTER 21

Alberto had been watching steadily from his third-floor window with the view of the hotel. He had become restless and had begun to think that maybe something was going to happen out of his view. The Chemist had arrived earlier and they talked about a plan that would catch Garon, Jake, and Allison off guard. They just needed to know where they were going to be. He kept a steady eye on the hotel across the way.

The Chemist had brought everything he needed to do his job. He was efficient and all he needed was a time and place. He hoped that his time would come. Maybe with this job, the Boss would see fit to promote him. He sat in the motel chair contemplating the plan and how it would go. His thoughts turned to his promotion and he reminded himself all would be good except for one thing. That one thing would be Aberto. The Boss had always trusted Aberto and he would stand in the way of the Chemist becoming the number two man in charge of the largest drug cartel in the world. He began to think of a larger role than just to set off explosions from time to time.

"Aberto, do you have any idea how they are going to leave that hotel or when?" The Chemist asked.

"I don't, but knowing Garon, he would be too careful to walk. There will be a car somehow and somewhere and we should be able to follow. We need to watch the front and the back of the hotel while leaving our car close by. We can't wait around much longer," Aberto said. "They are going to move soon. I feel it"

"I have everything I need in my backpack and I am ready to move," The Chemist said as he got out of his chair. He looked Aberto in the eye for a short time. "This needs to work. It can't be like the last time where Jake messed up on the timing. He caused me to miss and that can't happen again. I don't usually miss."

"Yes, I know," Aberto said looking hard back at his fellow cartel member. He studied his face, seeing determination and tightness that showed his resolve. "We won't miss, we will have them where we want them."

Aberto felt the intensity of the Chemist begin to burn through his skin and into his blood. He was feeling the cold heart of a killer, not so much unlike his own heart. It was a stand-off between two heartless humans, neither one fully trusting the other, each one having their own agenda and each one wanting the spot in the cartel that only had room for one. First Lieutenant wasn't a job for two men, only one man could be second to the Boss. But right now, they needed each other to complete their mission. When it was over, each would watch the other very closely.

"Let's go," Aberto said. "I'll take the front side and you the back. Our car will be parked on the street. You see them get in a car, call and we meet at our car and follow."

"I have the rest covered," The Chemist said. "Just get us to the right place and I will eliminate the traitors."

They walked out disguised and packed with all the guns, ammo, and The Chemist's own arsenal that he was so adept at using. Each had to trust the other and once outside they had to believe that each would be true to their word. Each knew the other man wanted the job. But each had to be successful to even have a chance. This job had to happen with them cooperating with each other. The future would be handled in some other way, and they both knew that to be true.

Each man took their place hidden from view and watching the exits in the front and the back of the hotel. This was it. It was the start of what could be the most profitable act for both men. They waited in silence and concentrated. They could not miss.

——▲——

It was 6:00 pm and the car that Garon had arranged would be here soon. Garon was nervous and Branch was still putting on makeup. Jake was in the room with Allison, going over with her the plan for the meeting where the car would be left and what to do, and what to say to Anastasia. *Some meeting, Jake thought. Four people all on the run, looking over their shoulder at every turn. I had scary meetings before, but this one I have a bad feeling about. Really bad.*

Jake looked sadly at Allison as she finished putting on the makeup that could not hide the damage to her face. He felt badly for her, and he sometimes questioned his motives for staying with Allison. He knew that deep inside he loved her. He had protected her, nursed her to health, and remained possibly the only human being on the planet that could keep her under control. If not for him, Jake knew she would probably be dead right now. He had changed some through this relationship. He used to be "Shallow Jake", any woman would just not do. They had to be pretty and lively. But more recently, since Jake had taken her under his wing, she had become more to Jake. Her face had undergone so much that plastic surgery was starting to show ill effects on her. They had done their best, but the fire and the fact that this was her second surgery had marred her face and it was only a shell of its former beauty.

She had finished with her makeup and turned to Jake. "How do I look?"

"You look great, as you always did."

"Oh, thanks, Jake," she said, smiling at him with her eyes. Yes, those eyes that were still so captivating, so intense.

"You have always been pretty. I love that face," he said.

"Jake, you're so kind. I think I'm ready for this meeting. I'm a bit nervous, especially about the Boss and Aberto. They have something planned for me, I know it, I sense it."

"Relax," Jake replied. "I think Garon has the right plan, we meet with Anastasia, and get the money. After that, we can hide out wherever we please. Here, take your pills."

He handed her the water and pills and she took them and closed her eyes, as if that made her better on the spot. In her own mind, Jake knew she wasn't ever going to be healed in her mind. Her mental health would always be a concern. But Jake was willing to overlook her faults and help her deal with it. If they can just finish this one job, all would be good and he would take care of Allison Branch. Just finish.

They came out of the bathroom together. Jake squeezed her hand for support. Garon was ready to go and he was becoming restless about the fact that Aberto was somewhere, possibly watching them right now. He was nervous.

"Let's go. The car is here to take us to The Deuce. Make sure you have everything and leave nothing behind," Garon said. "Be calm and don't get excited. Even if we run into the opposition, stay cool and don't panic."

The three of them walked outside and found the car with keys in it. Garon drove and they headed out of the parking lot, headed for The Deuce. Not far behind, the car driven by Aberto, was on its trail. Aberto stayed far enough behind as to not be noticed.

Garon pulled up in a parking spot along the street. They got out and locked the doors and headed towards the Deuce. Aberto pulled in to a parking lot across the street far enough away to be hidden but close enough for a view of Garon's vehicle. He let The Chemist out and he waited. This was going to work. The key was not to be seen or noticed. They had accomplished that. The plan was going to work.

CHAPTER 22

Marx and I had been through all of the pictures except one. Marx picked it up and studied it more closely than he had the others. He had a frown on his face that was telling me he had missed something from before and was just now picking up on it. I looked at it, too, and recognized the man as Oscar Stephenson, the guy that had gone missing years ago. It was the cold case we had started with that got us into the whole Allison Branch debacle.

"There's something strange about this picture," Andy said. "Something that I missed before."

"It's just a guy in a suit," I replied. "You probably just have had that picture in your mind from the cold case when it started."

"No, it's more, Mike."

"I don't get it," I said grabbing the picture to look closer. "Looks like the same picture we had all along."

"I know that you think it is," Andy said as he grabbed the picture out of my hand. "Look closer and you can see a picture of a family behind his desk. You see it?"

"Okay, yeah, I see it. But I can't make out the faces at all," I said

"We're going to get it blown up at the lab. Then try to make out who those two people are," Marx said still staring at the picture.

"Oh, no, wait, you're telling me it's not his sister in the photo?" I asked.

"I think I already know who it is. But let's get this photo blown up first and see exactly who it is," Marx said.

Confused, I sat there staring at him intensely. His mind worked so differently than mine. It was more relentless in his pursuit of what he was after. When Marx had a theory, he was going to the ends of the earth to prove it. I think I knew what his theory was and that in itself had me worried. Not for me or for Marx, but for Oscar Stephenson.

Marx gathered up his pictures and information and was heading down to the precinct with the picture in an envelope. At that moment Mike's phone signaled.

"Do you need to go somewhere?" Marx asked.

"No, I was supposed to call Margaret about an hour ago."

"How is she doing, by the way?"

"Okay, I guess. She's been going to a therapist."

"You want to ride along?" he asked.

"Sure, why not?"

▲

Margaret had been to a therapist at Mike's request. She had tried to participate, but whenever she got back home, she was once again alone in a world that she never asked for. To lose her husband and her daughter, both in ways that she had never imagined, was more than most people could handle.

On one side of her mind, she kept having the memories of Sheila as a small child, the memories of her smiles and tears that go along with growing up. Graduation, prom, and her marriage to Mike. Each day, Margaret ran through Sheila's life a little at a time almost every day. Those memories flooded back to her, and she could not escape them, nor did she want to. It was all she had left.

On the other hand, Margaret had the rough memories of Jerry and his antics. She had loved him at one time and had this beautiful child with him. But he moved on from Margaret and had the sordid affair, leaving her alone so often, especially after Sheila had died. He had become a monster over a short period of time, someone she despised but yet hung onto. It was how she grew up in her generation. No matter how bad, you stay together. Divorcees was just taboo for her. Divorcees were talked about and shunned, and Margaret had been brought up that way. She had told her therapist that there were endless days of nothingness.

Her therapist had suggested a hobby, something that would keep her mind off the past and let her be in the here and now. Mike had suggested one for her, and upon his advice, started her hobby. She enjoyed it and it only took an hour out of her day. Every time she went, she became more energized. It was not the therapist that was helping her so much, but her new hobby gave her a new sense of purpose. *Thank you, Mike. Thank you...*

▲

The Chemist was done. His work was easy and he

was on his way back to the car. Aberto had waited for him and as he walked towards him, he wondered if he could trust this man. He had always done his work well for the Boss and had never ever crossed the cartel. They had to complete this mission and all would be good, for now.

Jeremy slipped into the passenger seat where he could view the scene. He and Aberto had planned and prepared and, of course, Jeremy knew that he, "The Chemist", was the best. Aberto knew it, too, and all he could do right now was wait. He kept his eye on Jeremy as Jeremy was focused in on the scene ahead. His stare was fixed and almost in a strange way, content. This worried Aberto because he himself had always been moody, itchy, and restless. He never seemed to find his place in this world of dirty violence. But he understood just how much Jeremy Todd had been comfortable in that same world. That made Jeremy Todd very dangerous to Aberto. It made Jeremy Todd dangerous to everyone.

Aberto would have liked to hear the conversation that was taking place inside the bar. But, did it really matter? They were all going to die and that conversation would be their last. Anastasia, Jake the Traitor, Garon, and, of course, the crazy woman that everyone, including the Boss feared. She wasn't tougher than the Chemist or Aberto and certainly not tougher than the Boss. But she just had a way about her that exuded invincibility. She was like a spoiled child that could get her way. She always had known what she wanted and how she was going to get it. Allison Branch was indeed the deadliest of them all because she knew exactly how to manipulate people. She just had to go. Today.

▲

Inside the bar, Garon, Jake, Anastasia, and, of course, Allison were sitting at a round table in one of the darker areas of the bar. Garon was nervous and could not keep his head from turning in all directions. It was 6:45 and they had each had one drink in front of them. Allison was the smartest one sitting with her back to the wall, where she could see everything. She had done this in most places she had been in due to habit. Jake sat next to Allison on her right and Anastasia was directly across from Allison, her back to the door. Garon was on Allison's left.

They all had made it there not really knowing if they were detected or not. They had risked much to be here, but it was all for the money which Anastasia and Allison needed desperately. Anastasia needed the money for her mother's treatment, Allison and Jake needed it to survive, and Garon, well, he figured he would get his cut for helping and then he would disappear.

"Look," Anastasia said, looking around the table one by one. "Here is our situation. I know where our contact is and we will need to get there to at least get our money. He gets a cut as Andres had wanted him to do that favor for him. We make a deal today on how to split it now, not later. Otherwise, we have no deal and the money stays where it's at. Andres left a letter with directions on how to split the money. Here is the way he has it and that's the way we should leave it."

Allison just nodded her head as she looked through Anastasia as if looking deep into her soul. Allison didn't really trust her, but she had to hold on to what Andres' wishes were. Garon was quiet and intently focused on each word and Jake was intently focused on Allison.

"Agreed," Allison said after taking a sip of her

vodka martini. "We all know the contact and his name is William Montaldo. Anastasia, you know where he is, so why don't you let us know where and we'll head out of here?"

"We have to agree on the cuts first. Here is what I have," Anastasia said pulling out the paper she had scribbled on. She started to lay out the numbers, but the waiter interrupted, asking if they needed another drink. They each waved him off and he made his way back to the bar. The waiter went behind the bar and into the back room, pulling out his phone along the way. He dialed the phone and Aberto answered on the other end.

"They are here," the waiter said.

"Good, keep an eye on them. If they get up to leave, you call me," he said quickly. "No mistakes."

"Got it," the waiter replied and hung up the phone and pulled the wad of cash from his pocket and stared at it. It was more money that he made in a month working at *The Deuce*.

Back at the round table, the cuts had been agreed upon. Garon had his doubts about this whole process. He had felt under the table for bugs and trusted no one in the place. Even the waiter was starting to look familiar. He had been in situations like this before that had blown up in his face. He had survived and had done so because of his intuition. Garon thought ahead and tried to see any speed bumps in their way. The biggest one was Aberto. He had to be around somewhere, and Garon knew how good Aberto was at hunting his target. It was like feeling his way around in the dark, making sure there were no traps laid along the way. He was feeling his way through this scene and usually his feelings were accurate.

Garon looked at the characters around the table and questioned himself on what he was doing hooked up with them all. He was becoming somewhat disengaged with the conversation and began to study each individual. He had known them all at one time or another and he wondered what they were like before they all entered a world of crime, deceit, sex, drug trafficking, and murder.

Could they all have been destined for this life? This life, where trust and mistrust mingled with what each of them had in common, was a bad childhood. Surely, it wasn't what they dreamed about as young children. Poverty and abuse had at one time or another formed their outlook on life. They had two thoughts in common. One, is that they were never going to be poor again. They vowed that one day they would never have to worry about their next meal or where they would sleep. That was a matter that money would take care of. Two, they would all four never again be abused and used by others and that flame burned brighter than the first. It's what gave them their will to survive and as he looked around the table at each victim of abuse, he saw in their eyes what had been in his and Aberto's eyes as children. Even as early teenagers in the slums, he and his brother had that look. They were thirsty for something more than what life had given them. What it came down to was that they each wanted to be loved and cared for. Deep down what they all wanted was redemption, and when they could not seem to get that, they had turned to their best form of relief. **Revenge**. It was clear to him now and he realized what they all were. It started to make more sense to him why they had all gravitated to each other, through circumstance or by chance. The birds of a feather had now flocked together. Each adult sitting at the round table had the same thoughts in mind. All different circumstances and even different countries they grew up in, yet they were birds of a feather that now as adults had come to see the world as owing them something, and they would get that no matter what it took. The young and wild Jake, coming from the same slums that Garon did. The hooker from Miami, that took to the streets and the world of prostitution to find someone, anyone that would love her. Then, there was Branch.

Garon had studied her carefully and right at this moment, he felt sorry for her. The scars had left her not nearly as pretty as before. She wasn't ugly from the scars, but she wasn't anything like she used to be. He knew that bothered her, but even so, she still carried with her that one, uncanny characteristic that had controlled so many. Those eyes, those controlling eyes were still there. Silvery, steel blue and intense, those eyes were her way in this mean and tough world she had known since childhood. Garon silently was rooting for her. He wondered how someone could live through her life and not be that crazy. *Are we all crazy?*

At that moment, Garon thought of telling Allison something he knew. That something would surely throw her into a different revenge track that could really help them escape the cartel. It would change her direction and her target from Mike Parsons to this one person in the cartel. He turned it over in his mind and thought that if he could just get her away from the others, for just a minute, he could tell her. Asking her to come away from the table would cause suspicion among the others.

Garon excused himself from the table and stopped by the bar for a pen. He went to the restroom and on a paper towel he wrote to her what he wanted to tell her. He would hand it to her when he got back. It would be easy to pass her the note as he was sitting next to her at the table. In his mind, he was doing the right thing, why, exactly at this time, he was going to do this, he didn't know. But something told him it was right. Garon had done a lot wrong in his life, but for right now, he would do something right. He wondered if this was what redemption felt like.

CHAPTER 23

Marx and I arrived at the lab to look at the photo he had blown up for him. We went back to the room and the package of photos were delivered by another young officer. Andy grabbed the photos quickly and we sat at the table as he emptied them out on the desk.

Looking at the photos closely, Andy Marx was rubbing his chin, as he did when he was concentrating.

"Look at these photos closely, Mike. Tell me what you see," he said.

I studied them momentarily and nothing was catching my eye. "I really can't see what you're looking for," I said. "I can see a picture of a little girl and a lady in the background."

"Look closer at the girl," Andy said.

I looked more thoroughly. Something about the girl was significant, but I couldn't put my finger on it. Suddenly, it hit me. It was her eyes, the blown-up picture had exposed what Andy Marx had been thinking and it was now clear to me, too.

"It's Branch," I whispered. "Holy shit, it's her." Those eyes, even as a child, were wicked, evil, even hard. A child in a picture not smiling was rare. But the photo was unmistakably, Allison Branch. Oscar Stephenson was her father. "But why the name change?" I asked.

"Her mom took her maiden name, Branch, back when Oscar left," Marx said. "She told me that when we worked together. She never told me her dad's name, just that her mom took her name back and she had her name legally changed. Now, the story she told me makes so much sense."

"What story?" I asked.

"When she was a girl, her mom took her to the arboretum in Downers Grove, just outside of Chicago, to play. She said she loved trees. She was always fond of the one in the play area. She said she could reach the low branches and loved to climb on it. They went there usually after an episode by her drunk father, when he came home and abused them. It was her mom's way of making it up to her for not being strong enough to kick him out or call the police," Marx said.

"This is all making so much more sense. It even makes me feel sorry for her," I said.

"I wouldn't let my guard down, Mike. You can't feel sorry for her now. She's a wanted fugitive and a killer," Andy said looking at me intently. "You know what she is and don't let yourself see her as the victim. It's what she wants. You start feeling that way and you become easy prey. She's fooled me and she's fooled you. You can't let her do that again," Marx said almost scolding me. "If she wants to take this opportunity to kill me, you know she can kill you, too."

"Stephenson is our cold case, but he may still be

alive. We get to him and then we might be able to get to her. If he's dead, then we have nothing to go on. But, if he is still alive, he may be the scent that we need to follow her trail," I said wishing Marx hadn't scolded me like that. I still felt sorry for her even though Marx had told me not to. I knew he was right, but all that abuse, no child should have to endure that. It was just my personality to feel badly for her.

Every time in my life when I thought I was doing someone a favor or was lending them a helping hand, it would blow up in my face. Like the old saying, "no good deed goes unpunished," I felt like I couldn't help myself. I wasn't tough enough to stand by and let something go without trying to solve someone else's problem. I could have always walked away from this, but remembering when Andy asked me if I could pull the trigger, I could not answer and this was probably the reason why I was feeling conflicted about Allison after all she had done.

That's right, just fix everyone else, I couldn't fix Sheila, I couldn't fix Branch, can't seem to fix Margaret either. I must not have anything to offer anyone. That's a sad realization, my friend.

"Mike! Hey Mike!"

I shook out of the thoughts and heard his barking voice. "Yeah, I'm here," I mumbled. "I just drifted off for a second."

"Look, you need to focus here. If you're on my team, I need you at one hundred percent," Marx said.

"Okay, right. My fault for drifting off. I'm in," I said with so little confidence.

Like everything else, going in blind, I just went by the seat of my pants here. I mostly overthought most things and this was no exception but just having thoughts and not having a plan is a dangerous thing. And I was once again going to get into dangerous things. Once again, I had no idea of why I was doing this.

She asked again in my head, "Mike, do you believe in destiny?"

"Well, Allison, not before, but now, well, yes, I do."

Oh, the way I think...

—▲—

Allison had the note in her hand and had not yet read it. She placed it on the table with her hand over the top of it. Garon was trying to tell her something, but she couldn't read it in front of the rest. She had to wait.

"Look, we all know the cuts and the procedure," Jake said. "I think it's time to get out of here and plan for the trip to Chicago. The car is waiting in the street. Remember, straight to the car without delay. I don't trust Aberto and he could have eyeballs on us. We need to be quick and we need to get out of this town as soon as possible," Jake said as he stood up. "Time to go. I'll pay the tab."

Jake went to pay the tab, while Garon and Anastasia waited next to Allison. Jake came back and they started to walk out of The Duece, very close together.

"I've got eyes on four people headed to the car." Aberto said. "All is going according to our plan."

Just then a large city bus blocked their view. "Get that bus out of the way," the Chemist mumbled.

On their way out, Allison remembered she had forgotten the note that Garon had given her.

"Jake, I forgot something on the table. I'm going back to get it," Allison said

"Wait, I'm going with you," Jake told Allison. To

Garon he said, "Allison left something inside. Go on to the car and get it started and pick us up at the entrance," Jake said sounding stressed by this inconvenience.

Allison and Jake walked back in the door and towards the table. When they got there, Jake grabbed the note off the table and stuck it in his pocket.

"Let's go, I don't feel good about this. We need to get out of here," Jake said as they started back toward the door.

Back at the car, Garon had tried to start it, but it wouldn't turn over. He left Anastasia in the car and went to check underneath the hood.

As soon as Garon had started to lift up on the hood of the car, he thought of the note he had left for Allison. Yes, of course, that was my good deed, my redemption. It was his last thought on this earth. The flash in front of his eyes was brilliant and the explosion was deafening. It was his last living sight and sound.

Jake and Allison had just started to open the door and they both saw the radiant flash of light and the loud, booming noise. Immediately Jake thought, *Chemist, damn Aberto!* It made Allison think *Andres!* They both knew instinctively to run. They ran back inside and out into the back alley. They ran fast, darting in and out of the back alleys that Jake was familiar with.

Aberto and the Chemist had done their job, or so they had thought. Aberto's phone rang and he immediately answered. It was the waiter inside The Duece.

"Aberto, they went out the back. They are running for it through the alleys," the waiter said hurriedly.

"Who ran out the back? What do you mean?" Aberto said in a panicked voice.

"Jake and the girl, they left something inside and they came back in to get it. Then the explosion happened."

Damn it, the bus, the bus got in the way! It must have gotten in the way of seeing them go back in.

"We have to get going. Jake and the girl went back inside when the bus went by. We missed them and the waiter said they went out the back through the alleys," Aberto told the Chemist.

"How? The Chemist asked. We saw all four head out of the bar. That couldn't have happened!"

"The bus got in our way," Aberto told him.

"I must have looked away from the front, I didn't see any bus!" the Chemist shot back at Aberto.

"Well, you just missed it, but after the bus left, all I could see was the car and the explosion," Aberto said.

They both were thinking the worst. The Boss was not going to like this.

Aberto screeched his tires as he turned the car into the back alleys behind The Duece. In front, black, boiling smoke was rising from the car as the flames engulfed only two of the four targets. Sirens were blaring and the local cops and SWAT were on the scene quickly. Aberto sped into the alley, flying at a dangerous speed, flirting with their own demise as they looked hurriedly for Jake and Branch on foot.

The Chemist shouted, "There! They're jumping the fence. Aberto drew his gun and fired missing them before they hit the ground running. "Shit, they're getting away!" Aberto exclaimed. The Chemist quickly got out of the car and drew his own gun after leaping the fence. He ran hard down the alley and Aberto drove the car towards the end of the next alley, hoping to cut them off. He halted the car at the end of the alley and got out of the car and drew his gun running in the direction of the Chemist. Surely, they would find them, they had to have them closed in from both directions. But all they found was each other.

Jake and Allison had busted inside a door to the apartment in the alley and held the gun to the occupant's head.

"Nobody makes a sound, do you understand?" Jake asked the hostage.

The man only shook his head and made no noise as he was sweating profusely like his captors. Allison peeked through the curtains and saw Aberto and the Chemist run back toward the alley exit and get in their car. Aberto hit the gas and they were gone. Allison and Jake had to move, and they were ready to exit the alley and head on foot to the Amtrak station. Aberto and the Chemist weren't far behind and she and Jake needed to get far, far away from this scene.

Jake turned towards the man and pointed the gun with the silencer attached at the man's face. His shot was true and right to the middle of the man's forehead. The man dropped instantly. Jake showed no mercy as this man would have been a witness and he could not afford to let him go. Allison Branch did not flinch. This was her world, cold, calculated, and full of death. Death no longer fazed her and she had no fear of it at all. The craziness that was Allison Branch had once again taken over from a new catastrophe. Garon and Anastasia were dead, the Chemist and Aberto were on their trail, hunting them down, and Jake had just killed a complete stranger, who could no longer identify them. All seemed quite normal to Allison. She thought that now she was back in her perfect world. She felt almost nothing at all, except for one burning thought and that thought was that she wouldn't have been here at all if it wasn't for that bastard, Mike Parsons.

They quickly found a cab, and Jake instructed the

driver to head to Anastasia's address. They were going to head somewhere, anywhere, just very far from here. They would need her vehicle to get away. They had to regroup and they needed essentials like food, more clothes, and extra disguises. Jake had all of that going in his mind, but Allison could only stare out the window and think of what she was going to do next. Sirens were loud and even those screeching noises could not bring her out of her trance.

I wonder what if Mike Parsons had picked me. Would I be happy? Would we have really fallen in love? I won't ever know because he never gave me the chance. Not even the time of day. He was it; all that I had wanted. All he had to do was respond. But, oh, no, he had to head out of the bar with that bimbo. He didn't pick me. Why? I was so pretty that he just had to pick me, right? WRONG! No, nobody ever picked me! Mike, the department, my father, not anyone, except for my mom and she was so weak. Even she couldn't save me from myself. I feel that spirit again, that wild spirit of blood rushing through my veins, the only feeling that ever made me feel alive. I was not pretty anymore, not even close to what I was before the explosion. But they are all going to pay. Every last one of them will feel my revenge. Every...single...one!

CHAPTER 24

Andy Marx and I were about to leave the station when his phone rang. He answered quickly, listened, and hung up.

"I've been informed by a couple of our agents that there's been an explosion at *The Deuce* in Miami," FBI agent Jenna Holmes said. "There are two bodies in a car, blown up. They talked to the workers in the bar and said that there were four people in the bar and that two of them were in the car when it exploded and two others had come back to get something. After the explosion, those two ran out the back of the bar."

"Did they get a description of the two?" Marx asked.

"Yes," Holmes replied. "From the description, it looks like it might be our girl, Branch, and her boy, Jake Benson. The owner said that the girl had scars, maybe from burns and the guy was young and fit the description of Jake."

Marx paused, rubbing his forehead with his palm. I

knew immediately something big was up.

"Look, we have a couple of things to get together here," Marx said. "Keep us informed and we will alert people here."

"It will be on the news all over the country tonight," Holmes said. "This could be the time that the cartel really made a mistake. It could be the break we are looking for. They couldn't have gotten too far. We're going to cover all the airports, bus stations, and Amtrak."

"Okay, good," Marx replied. "Any idea of which way they were heading?"

"Not yet, but one more thing," Holmes said. "The guy that worked their table was really nervous. I feel like he knows something, and we're going to hold him for questioning. I'll let you know what we find out from him."

"And one more thing," Holmes added. "The local cops found a body, in a house in the back alley. Shot in the forehead with a Sig Sauer Mosquito with a silencer. Close range kind of kill an assassin would do."

"That gun is discontinued, right?" Marx asked.

"Right, which would lead possibly to the cartel and possibly Jake," Holmes said.

"Okay, great. I'll be waiting for your call," Marx said disconnecting the call.

I looked at Marx, knowing it was about HER. "Okay, where is she?" I asked.

"She's in the states. Not sure where exactly but she's trying to leave Florida, possibly with Jake. The description, and it will be on the news tonight, Jenna Holmes said," Marx said tapping his pen on the desk. "I'm just not sure. We'll have to check the news feeds tonight. See the artist description and we will know for sure."

I looked up slowly at Marx. "She's coming here, isn't she?" I asked looking back down at my feet and then looked back up for my answer.

"I'm not sure, and neither is the FBI. We need to wait to see what Chrisler and Holmes find out. The news and what else they provide from questioning a key witness will be important. For now, we just have to sit tight and wait."

Yep, sit and wait. Sit and wait for HER to kill me!

Jake and Allison rushed from the taxi to Anastasia's apartment. Jake tried to be cool, but he knew that Aberto and The Chemist were going to follow quickly. So would the cops or maybe even the FBI, maybe even the Boss. These were not stupid people and they would be after them soon. With Allison Branch by his side, Jake picked the lock and went inside. They only had a few minutes for departure so they headed quickly to find the keys to her vehicle. Jake feared that they would soon be caught. Luckily, the keys were in plain sight on the kitchen table.

Allison was breathing hard and Jake tried to put his hand on her shoulder to calm her. This would be no easy task to escape. He looked out the window of the apartment and spotted them, the Boss, Aberto, and The Chemist, coming down the street towards the apartment. Aberto knew this was the neighborhood where Anastasia lived but not the exact apartment number. They got out of the car, guns drawn, Jake and Allison were not getting away this time.

Jake had spotted Anastasia's car from the third-floor window. At the same time, he heard Allison scream that they had been found. Jake panicked and knew they had to hurry out the back. They had just made it, and he felt the cockiness that he had always carried coming back to him now. He had always had that until recently and the scene at *The Deuce* had made him feel that his end was near. The explosion easily could have taken his and Allison's lives, but they escaped. Now, he had another dilemma.

It was the note Jake thought. The note had saved them from the fiery inferno that was the work of the The Chemist. It had to be Aberto and The Chemist working together to kill them all. Aberto had his very own brother killed! If Aberto could kill his brother for the Boss, why would he stop now? They were in grave danger and would be until I can kill them. I have to. It was now kill or be killed and that was an absolute truth. I can run now, but at some point, if Allison and me will survive, it will because we play offense and not defense. I have to think. The note, I have to read the note. But not now, not in front of Allison.

Jake reached into his pocket and felt the note. He would read it later but the curiosity was killing him. Just like it had almost done before in South America. *Read it later*...Andres had taught him the lesson about his impetuous behavior before. He would not make the same mistake again. Andres had taught him many things and now he would put them to use. He was ready to step in to some big shoes. His father's shoes.

Aberto and the others went inside the gate of the apartments. Jake had to think quickly, checking the area out the back, Jake saw that if they went out the back steps and into the back alley, they could go down a block and get to the car.

They quickly left the apartment and went down the steps. Jake and Allison could hear their voices. Jake held his finger to his lips to hush Allison while he grabbed her hand and started to run. They ran swiftly to the next block and turned up the alley. Jake hoped he calculated the distance correctly. When they made it to the street, it was right there in front of them. Quickly, they got into the car and sped away.

Oscar, Aberto, and the Chemist had found the right apartment and broken in. They looked around and Aberto could not find anything that made them think they were here. They would wait for them as Aberto knew they would head here. Aberto knew they had few choices left without any money or means. They would have to come here.

CHAPTER 25

"Self-preservation is the first principle of our nature."-
Alexander Hamilton

*A*llison Branch thought of herself as a survivor. She had always thought of herself first and she felt she didn't need to explain that to anyone. The things she had experienced in her life made her think that no one could do anything to her that was worse than what she had already endured. It was what had made her the most dangerous person that I had ever met. Knowing this, I had little time and I had to call Katy. She needs to know.

As Marx had told me to sit tight and wait, I was on my way home with my own thoughts. I had to call Katy as soon as I got home, but for now I had to think of the right thing to say. Although I had seen a much tougher Katy through my last experience with her taking care of me after my two-day drunk, she was still easily spooked by the thought of ever having to face Allison again. There was no question that no matter how much stronger Katy was getting, there was one demon out there that could haunt her, make her have nightmares in the daytime, and cause her to break out in cold sweats. That demon was Allison Branch.

I pulled into my drive and hurried inside. I shut off the alarm and took off my jacket and laid it on the couch. I sat down and debated with myself about giving any information to Katy, but, somehow, I felt that she was my partner. Just like Marx, we had been through many things together that had changed us and made us feel alike. Even though the three of us had handled these things in our own way and survived, we had our own way of walking away from the fire we had just walked out of. Twice! All three of us had adjusted differently and the people we are now is not the people we were before. We had changed in our own distinct ways. Some ways for the better and some ways for the worse. For sure, each of us had a different level of recovery and for what all these past events had meant to us and how we felt, each of us were not at the same place. I looked at my phone and punched in Katy's contact information. I stared at her number for a while and soon caused me to be in a trance. I did not dial as my thoughts went back, way back.

I saw myself, the failed prosecuting attorney, sitting in a bar while my suffering wife was at home, once again. There was a brunette sitting in the bar and I made some small talk with her, but had moved on to another interest after about fifteen minutes. The brunette was pretty. Her eyes of steel blue had captured my interest, but she seemed shy. She just didn't seem to be my type, but those eyes had burned something in to me that, at the time, had no real meaning to me except that I not just saw them, I felt them. I remember thinking how strange that made me feel at that time, but I moved on because she just didn't seem like I was getting anywhere with her. Why didn't I see that when I met her the second time? I missed it and once again, my cockiness and ego let something slip by that was almost fatal. Yes, that is how it all started. The hate and anger that so much filled her heart was just egged on by my own rejection of her. First her father, then the academy, then Sheila, all had rejected her. It was the beginning of her rampage, not only to destroy me, but a long list of people associated with me, so that I would suffer along the way to my own demise. SHE had killed Sheila, I was sure of it and so was Margaret. Jerry was killed in the process, too, destroying Margaret's life.

At this point, I knew I was asleep, as I knew I was forcing myself to wake up from this bad dream. But I couldn't wake up. I felt like I was watching a movie and all the characters were flashing in front of my face like the credits at the end. The screen said, "The Dead." There was Sheila, Jerry, Breanne, Henry Hannah, Andrea Stephenson Raines, Andres Montoya and multiple others. I tried to get out of my seat and leave the theater, but I couldn't as I pushed down hard on the handles of my chair, trying to raise my body up, but it was frozen. I opened my mouth to yell out, but no words would come. Then, the new faces started shooting across the screen and some of the others in the theater began to laugh. I saw them all so clearly. The screen said, "The Survivors." There was Marx, Margaret, Katy, followed by my brother, James. Then there was Brenda Jackson, Oscar

Stephenson, Jake Benson and Carrianne Martinez. Then across the screen came Joanna, tears in her eyes, and then there was me, in a hideous photo of shock and fear, my own picture flowing slowly across the screen, the laughter started to get louder and more intense and the chant began, "Mikey! Mikey! Mikey!" as the clapping and stomping became thunderous. When the noise had reached its height, it all of a sudden stopped...the last face slowly began to appear on the screen, a woman I think, long blonde hair covering her face.

"Hello, Mikey!!" she shouted. Her hair suddenly flew up and uncovered her face. That face now turned up and looking right at me, those eyes, blue and sharp, her face covered with scars that were ugly and the demon that was HER, had now appeared.

She only said one more word. "WHY?"

I suddenly woke and I was sweating profusely, just like all the other dreams I had before. I looked down at my phone and keyed in my password and saw my home screen. It was now 1:00 am and calling Katy now was out of the question. I got up slowly from the couch and felt totally exhausted. I shuffled back to the shower. The warm water felt good and somehow it calmed my nerves just a little. These dreams, they had to stop or else I may just go crazy. Or, had I already done so?

I finished my shower and wrapped my towel around me and headed for the kitchen. Maybe a good shot of whiskey would do the trick? Or maybe two or three? I reached for the bottle, and I heard the doorbell ring. I set the bottle back in the cabinet and went to the front door. I checked through the peep hole and saw it was Marx. I quickly let him in.

"I called twice and got no answer, so I thought I

would check on you," Marx said.

"I guess I was sleeping hard. I didn't hear it," I responded, not wanting to tell him of my dream. He would surely think I was crazy and Marx didn't need to think that about me right now. "Let me get some sweats on and a T-shirt."

I quickly changed and came back to the living room and Marx cut right to the chase, as he always did. He didn't waste much time at anything.

"Look, I got a call from Chrisler an hour ago," Marx started. "He let me know that during the explosion at *The Deuce,* Anastasia and a thug named Garon that worked for the cartel they were chasing were killed. The explosion was meant for all four of them. They interviewed the waiter at *The Deuce,* and he told them he was paid by Garon's brother, Aberto, to watch the four and let him know when they left. Aberto and possibly the bomber went after Branch and Jake. Looks like Branch and Jake are on their own and, according to the waiter, are heading to Chicago, possibly about money. The best the FBI can figure is that they made it out of town and if the cartel catches up with them first, they would surely kill them both."

"I guess we can add this to the credits at the end," I mumbled.

What are you talking about?" Marx questioned.

"Well, nothing, we just have a long list of the dead and a list of the survivors. I meant nothing by it, really..."

"No, wait," Marx interrupted. "The list of survivors, we have to focus on that list. Surely there is one on that list that will screw up."

"Maybe," I responded, feeling the guilt of not telling Marx my dream just because I felt scared by it and I didn't want him to think I didn't have the guts for this. "But don't forget, sometimes, someone on the list of the dead can help the most."

"You may be right, my friend," Marx answered. "You just may be right."

▲

Allison and Jake had made it safely out of Miami and were now alone together in a dumpy motel on the outskirts of Atlanta. They needed rest and time to sort things out. The beds were small with outdated furniture. It was not a very good neighborhood, but one that hid them well. They had very little with them and this was hard for any woman. She needed new clothes, more make-up, and more meds. She had very little left, just one bottle and Jake knew that would not be enough. Jake knew that they couldn't stay long so he got right to the point.

"Here's what we are facing. Garon and Anastasia are dead, Aberto and The Chemist are surely on our trail, and the FBI won't be far behind. You and I both need new clothes and we need better disguises. We've got to ditch our guns and get new when we get to Chicago. Once we get that money, we need to disappear and Andres had taught me how to do that," he said seemingly in one breath.

"Jake, we also need to stay out of airports and Amtrak. We have to find a different route to travel and get to Milwaukee. We have lots of connections there. We can re-stock everything before we get to Chicago and collect our money," Allison said.

Jake liked the sound of *OUR* money. He thought he could really like this woman and with their new money, he would make sure she got the right medical attention for her face, a new face with which she would be happy.

"I agree, tomorrow we leave for Milwaukee. We

only have one disguise left each. We need to keep it until we get to Milwaukee. Then, we can change it up and go with the older person look. I think we'd look good in gray hair," Jake said winking at Allison. "Between now and then, you need rest. Try and get some sleep and we will leave about 4:00 am," Jake said walking by her bed to touch her arm lightly and reassure her.

"We're going to be okay, right, Jake?" she asked.

"We'll be fine and don't worry and get some rest," Jake said.

He walked to the bathroom so that he could read the note in his pocket. He unfolded the note written on a paper towel. He read the note silently:

Allison,

I really didn't want to have to tell you this, but all along Oscar Stephenson has been working with the cartel. It was never our intention to let you see him. I thought that you deserved to know. But the Boss had talked to Oscar and to keep working with us, he wanted Oscar to kill you.

He's still out there, somewhere with Aberto and the Boss. Their mission is to kill you. I will protect you as much as I can. But Jake, if he finds out, he will go after Stephenson, possibly kill him.

Allison, Oscar Stephenson is your father. Garon.

Jake read the note to himself once more. *Her father, all along he was working with us. Cutthroats, all of them! She will never see this note, not if I have anything to do with it.*

Jake folded the note up and put it back in his pocket. He knew exactly what Allison would have done and then, they would surely be caught. She was too reckless, and he was becoming much more calculating. He would have a plan to take care of Allison's father. Oscar Stephenson would go down.

Jake just couldn't allow Allison to kill her father. He would do it himself. They would get the money and be free and he would finally have Allison. But first, he needed to make a call. He pulled out his phone and dialed the number...

CHAPTER 26

Sometimes, someone on the list of the dead can help the most.

The Chemist knew that his days were numbered if he stayed with this group. This was his second screw up and his time with the cartel was running short. He had made up his mind while he and Aberto and Oscar Stephenson were driving on the road together tracking the two defectors, Allison Branch and Jake Benson. Aberto had known what Anastasia's car looked like and the Boss had some cops on the payroll who looked up the license plate and they knew exactly what kind of car they were looking for, a black Mercedes, not a simple find as there are several out there, but having the license plate number would help. When they found their prey, his troubles would start and he had no plans to be with them when this happened. He, in fact, would be long gone and he would disappear. He knew how to do just that. In this line of work, you could make one mistake, not two, and he wasn't going to be killed by the Boss or any of his lieutenants. He had finally had enough of this work and he had enough money stashed away to make a new life. He had made the one kill he needed to make and that was enough. He kept his plan alive in his head as they neared Atlanta.

"We need to stop soon, it's about as far as I can go right now without a little rest," Aberto said.

"Yeah, I'm tired too," Oscar said as he stretched and yawned. "We can't be that far behind them. I hate for us to give them more time."

Jeremy did not respond as he was busy planning in his head. Next stop he would disappear, and he knew how he was going to do it.

"Hey, I got to take a leak," The Chemist said. "Why don't you pull over and gas up and we can keep after them. I'll drive for a while."

"Okay," Aberto said, "I need some rest and a stretch too. We can't take long. They are still ahead of us."

"There's a station at this exit," Oscar said. "Let's pull over there."

The car pulled into the station and Aberto got out and began to put gas in the car while Oscar and The Chemist went inside. The Chemist watched as Oscar went to get a coffee, he walked towards the restroom area and slipped into the women's room, not the men's room. He looked up and saw what he was hoping for, a drop ceiling. He climbed up on the stall and pushed the ceiling tile up and to the side. There wasn't much room up there, but just enough for him to pull himself out of view and replace the tile. Now, he just had to wait. He held onto a metal pipe in the ceiling and he had left a small opening in the tile he replaced to see when the coast was clear. He was sweating but he had had been in hiding places before and he had the patience to wait this out. Two women came into the bathroom and he looked away from the opening. He was a lot of things, but he wasn't a Peeping Tom. He closed the tile slowly. He listened for them to leave and then opened the tile just a hair to see if they came looking for him.

Aberto had finished putting gas in the car and he had come inside to pay.

"We're ready, where is The Chemist?" asked Oscar as they walked towards the door.

"I don't know, he went to the can and I didn't see him come out. Maybe he's still in there," Oscar replied.

"We need to check on him," Aberto said and they walked to the restroom area.

They went inside the men's room and there was no one there. Aberto started to panic. "Check the women's, quick."

Oscar went in the women's and walked around and there was no one there either. The Chemist watched from behind the small crack in the tile. He wanted to make sure he left and gave them time to leave before he got down.

"No one in there," Oscar said as he walked back into the men's room.

"Damn it, he's cutting out on us," Aberto said as they walked out. "Are there side doors here?" he asked.

"Yeah, over there," Oscar said as they both hurried towards the door.

They walked out the side door and nothing. No one anywhere to be seen. They hurried back to the car, just in case they missed him. He was not there.

"Get in," Aberto told Oscar. "We can't stay here any longer. He's cut and run and he will be hard to find, I'll call The Boss and let him know. We've got to stay on the trail or we may never find them."

Oscar and Aberto got in and started the car. He began to drive away, and he called the Boss immediately.

"We lost the Chemist. I think he's run on us. He's out."

"I'll take care of him. You guys stay after Allison and Jake. They are the ones I want for now. I'll deal with The Chemist later," the Boss replied.

"Okay, got it. We're on our way and just on the outskirts of Atlanta. They aren't too far ahead I'm sure," Aberto said.

Do whatever you have to do!" the Boss fumed. "I swear on my mother's grave, I will kill you all if you don't find them AND kill them," he hissed. "They can turn on us any minute and the only thing saving us right now is that cocky kid, Jake. He'll make a mistake. Now get moving."

"We're on our way," Aberto said and disconnected the call.

They hurried out of the gas station. Aberto looked out his rearview mirror and saw the cops pulling into the gas station. *Go, damn it! Just go already.*

The car hit the highway and Aberto hit the gas pedal and picked up some speed, their lives were at stake and their prey had a half hour jump on them. The car picked up speed and they soon were on the way. Two groups heading through Atlanta, both with the same objective. Survival...

▲

The Chemist had slowly lowered himself down from the ceiling to the stall in the women's room. He was nimble and quick in these situations as the Army had taught him well. He peeked out the door to see if he was clear to leave and he saw the two cops heading into the men's room. Once the door closed behind them, he walked towards the side door and walked out into the Atlanta, Georgia, night. The Chemist would disappear and with his backpack on his back, he began his journey to a place where he would never be found. He knew exactly where he was going, all he needed was a ride. He would get one and he would survive. He always had...

▲

I now had the task of letting Katy know what was going on. I dialed Katy's number and she answered on the second ring.

"Katy, this is Mike," I said.

"Mike, what time is it? What's going on?" Katy mumbled her questions as she was deeply asleep when he called.

"Look, I'd like to come over if I can. Can you put on some coffee and I can be there in twenty minutes?" I asked hurriedly.

"Of course, I'll get it going right now," she said started to wake up more.

"I don't want to say anything on the phone. I'll tell you when I get there."

"Okay, Mike, be careful," Katy said and hung up.

I dressed quickly and headed to my car. Once again, here I was, wrapped up in stuff I knew very little about. But there was no way I was going to let Katy hang out on her own right now. That dangerous woman is on the loose and Katy could be a target at any time. I headed to Katy's and my thinking went back to HER. Branch.

Why in the hell do I feel sorry for her? She's ruined so many lives and intends to ruin some more. All I have done is worry and not done anything about stopping her cold. I had to do something, but how? I had to lure her in somehow, or would she just come after me and I won't have to worry about that? So many questions and so many thoughts, yet, the main thing right now is protecting Katy. She needs me right now and I have to be strong and appear to be totally in control of myself, although on the inside, I knew that wasn't true. My mind is all over the place, but, right now, you need to focus, Mike. You just have to do this for you, for Marx and for Katy.

I was right on time, as twenty minutes from my house, I pulled into Katy's drive. I stopped the car and turned it off. I got out and headed up the sidewalk. *Focus! Right now.*

Katy answered the doorbell and at first, I was frozen by her clear and radiant smile. It was the one I had always noticed from my favorite bartender before, but now, it seemed different.

"Well, are you going to come in or just stand there?" Katy asked.

"Oh, um, sorry," I stammered. "I know I have seen that smile so many times, but this time, your beauty stunned me."

Katy flushed. I could feel this connection between us that I had always felt but also always denied. *No, not Katy, was my response to my thoughts. Something different now, something pulling at me.*

"Hey, it's good to see you again," I started. "Seems like a long time even though it was just a few days."

"Yeah, but I am so glad you are here. Do you want a drink?"

"No, no drink tonight, but we do need to sit and talk. There are some new things out there concerning Branch and I want to be sure I let you know and keep you in the loop," I said. Katy's smile turned quickly to a frown. "It looks like Branch and Jake are on their own. They barely escaped an explosion in Miami and are being hunted by the cartel and the FBI. The waiter at the bar they were at told the FBI they may be headed to Chicago and that there was money involved. Big money."

I didn't mean to be that blunt, but I figured we didn't have time to beat around the bush. Katy had grimaced, knowing that Branch was now on the loose and her face had now turned to grave concern.

"Mike, I have gotten tougher. I was learning to put her in the past, but now it seems like we have to live the nightmare for a third time? Katy asked.

"Right now, Katy, you're safe. I will make sure of it. But for now, it has to be locked doors, set alarms and call me any time you see suspicious things. Any time, day or night, call me," I said. "Marx and I are on this thing and they will get caught."

"Mike, how can you be sure?" she interrupted. "She always has her way of sneaking up on us and when we least expect it, she appears like that thief in the night, stealing our confidence and putting us in terrible situations. Now, I am really scared. We can't be that lucky three times!" she exclaimed getting up from her seat and pacing the room.

Now, Katy was becoming more emotional and I had to calm her. I got up from my seat and crossed the room to her. I grabbed her by the shoulders and turned her gently to face me.

"Katy, look at me. We've got to play smart and under control. I need you to be right there with me in spirit, but I will make sure you don't get in harm's way," I promised, not knowing if it was a promise I could keep, but I sure intended to keep Katy away from HER.

She put her arms around my waist and laid her

head on my chest. I was feeling her need to be protected, but I also was feeling her, totally and fully I felt her mind touching mine. I was sensing her need and it was something I had tried to avoid getting too sensitive about. *It certainly couldn't be Katy, could it? Yet, I was sensing that it was. That all along it was her. My bartender friend, my confidant, and the one that always made me smile and laugh when I was down the most.* I lifted her chin and her eyes met mine. At this very moment, I was feeling possibly what Katy had wanted me to feel all along, but I had tried to resist for all the right reasons. I could not resist any longer...

CHAPTER 27

Aberto and Oscar Stephenson had gone as far as they could go. They needed sleep and it was nearing dawn. They pulled into the nearest hotel and checked in. They had what they needed but were still without a clue of where Jake and Branch were at this time. They were good and Jake, that cocky little brother of Carrianne's, was good. He had learned much from Andres. This had frustrated Aberto over the years, as he wanted to be Andres' favorite, but there was always Jake. *"Jake, help with this, Jake go with me here, Jake I have a job for you," were always the words directed to Jake, never to me. I'll take care of that traitor, just like we did my brother and Anastasia.*

Oscar undressed and showered quickly. They would not be able to stay long. When he finished, he put his clothes back on and lay on the bed.

"We'll catch them," Aberto said. "You better get some sleep because we are leaving early. Just a couple of hours and we'll be on our way. There is no time to waste. The waiter told me Chicago and we need to get there by morning. If we could find them sooner, it would be all the better. That car won't be hard to find."

"Well, don't underestimate Branch. Jake is what Jake is, but she is the dangerous one," Oscar said contemplating what he was saying about his own daughter. "If you take her for granted, she will make you regret it."

Aberto wasn't scared of her. In fact, he had wanted to kill her and told himself he would do it at the first opportunity. Oscar could have killed her easily during her recovery, but he never tried, even when the Boss told us all that she was dangerous. Aberto had the feeling that Oscar could not do it, for whatever reason, and that he would have to kill her himself. Oscar would be baggage. He didn't feel he could count on Oscar because they had not grown up in the business together. Aberto had thoughts of killing Oscar, but for some reason, he thought he held some magical key to Branch, not even knowing why, just trusting his intuition. So, Aberto would keep him around. At least until he had Branch in the bag and his promotion to top lieutenant was complete. *Number two man in charge of the largest cartel in Brazil. That sounds good to me. Nothing was going to stop me from my blind ambition that I will rise to number two. I had already killed my own brother, and will kill Branch and Jake and even Oscar if I have the opportunity. But Jake and Branch, they were the real prey. Get them, and I have everything I ever wanted. The money, the women, the fame and most importantly, the recognition that I am a big, big man.* It was his narcissist ego more than anything that drove Aberto. Always talking down to others and always trying to show his superiority in thought and in physical deed. *Yes, to all on-lookers, I am one tough man.*

Oscar had drifted off to sleep and Aberto was going to go outside and check around one more time. He didn't trust Jake or Branch and even though they were chasing them, Aberto was a plotter and tried to think what his prey would do. He did not rule out that they would come back to eliminate Oscar and him. He thought of every angle. He stuck his gun in his shoulder holster and went outside to check...

Anastasia's mother was very ill and there was very little time left. Her cancer had finally become too much to fight. The hospice nurse had just seen the news the night before and the home health care company had been made aware of the fact that Anastasia, was in fact the daughter of this dying mother. They did not have the heart to tell her what had happened and time was short anyway.

They would allow her to go peacefully. The money would no longer be needed and Anastasia and her mother would now both be free of life's pain and anguish. She shut her eyes for the very last time and never awoke again. She was gone. Anastasia and her mother were together again. In spirit, they were two souls of the same body, both completely different, but yet the same. Re-united once more, this time with no more fear, no more pain, and no more worries.

Aberto saw nothing as he paced along the perimeter of the building, smoking a cigarette. He felt as though someone was watching him and he couldn't free his mind of either an attack by the Boss or by Branch and Jake. He couldn't shake the fact that right now, he was not the aggressor. It most cases he had been, but now he had to think in reverse once again. What would they do and where would they come from? If he didn't find them first and kill them both, the Boss would then eliminate him. The pressure was surely on Aberto to find them, but what if they got to him first? He would be ready and he would eliminate them. He had to as it was his own life at stake.

And then there was Oscar, the baggage that Aberto didn't seem to be able to eliminate. *I could kill him and dump him, but the Boss likes the guy, for what reason I don't know. But my hunt would be easier if I knew for sure they wouldn't come back for him.* Aberto was almost finished with his cigarette and he walked back to the door and let himself into the room. Oscar jumped as Aberto's noise woke him. It startled Aberto and he pointed his gun at Oscar, mostly out of reflex. Oscar froze and, for a second, he really thought Aberto might shoot him.

"Relax," Aberto said. "It was mostly out of reflex because you jumped. I'm not going to shoot you but I was just startled when you jumped. Another hour and we take off."

"Right, I'll get at least one more hour of sleep," Oscar said.

But neither man would sleep as they both did not trust the other. This was getting out of hand and they needed to find them soon. They knew they were going in the right direction. They were heading to Chicago and they would catch up to them. Jake and Branch had to sleep too. Possibly they would pass them and get to Chicago before them. Aberto's waiter had let him know it was the destination of the four inside the bar.

What Aberto did not know was that the FBI was heading that way, too. Who would get there first? They needed to find that car, the one that belonged to Anastasia. Aberto hoped for luck but he knew that chances were slim. His thoughts occupied his mind and it kept him awake, he had to watch Oscar. Killing him would be so much easier. If the Boss hadn't liked Stephenson so much, he would have done it already. He was in enough trouble with the Boss, he didn't need to make more. But still, he didn't sleep and he kept his eye on Oscar, who, himself, kept his eye on Aberto.

CHAPTER 28

A ndy Marx was sifting through his mail, when he came across an odd envelope with no return address that made him curious. He opened the envelope and inside was a letter typed on plain white paper. He read the letter slowly and began to understand who was the author of the letter. Although, there was no signature, he knew who had sent it. He re-read it once more...

Detective,

I think you will find this information helpful as you search for Jake and Allison. Please do not let the authorities know I sent this to you, as it is against my protection agreement. The address you need to get to if you are going to beat them there is 4151 East Park Street in Chicago. The man, William Montaldo, is the man Mr. Parsons saw on the gravel road, and William worked for Andres at the farm. Andres told me if anything ever happened to him, William would have money at this address.

I know ALLISON, and, of course, I know Jake, and they will want to get to that money as soon as possible. You will need to move quickly if you want to get them as I am sure they are on their way to collect.

You can do whatever you want with Branch, but please don't hurt Jake. Try to bring him in and he can help you catch the Boss. Please save Jake, he's all I have left.

I know I am taking a risk writing to you, but I had to take the chance to save him.

Marx thought for a minute and he tried to sort this letter out. *It had to be Carrianne, but she is taking a huge risk sending this. Is this some kind of trick or trap? Maybe I call Chrisler and Holmes and give this to them, and they would have the jump on them. Surely, they would bring her to justice and get Jake in safely. But I know I want to bring her in, right? This has been my case all along, not the FBI's, and, besides, Branch betrayed me. She damn near killed me! This is my job even though it is against my better judgement. I need to tell Mike...*

Marx wrote down the Chicago address as he looked around to see if anyone in the room was watching. He wanted to quit the force, that was for sure, but he wanted to go out on his own terms and not be forced out in shame for doing something wrong. This was his last chance to be the hero, and he had to make sure Carrianne stayed in witness protection. He folded the note and slipped it into his jacket pocket. He would leave with the note, and he would destroy it later. Right now, he had to call Parsons. They might just be taking a trip to Chicago.

▲

I woke up laying on my back with Katy's head on

my chest. Her soft breathing softly brushing across my chest made me afraid to move and disturb her. She seemed so peaceful and so calm, in fact, calmer than I had ever remembered. *She felt protected. Imagine that, me protecting anyone. But this felt different and this was just more than one of my casual plays. I really felt her and her feelings for me. Or, was it just what I was wanting to feel justified sleeping with Katy when all along I had told myself that I wouldn't? Ever. Or was this where Branch's old friend, "Destiny" made the scene? I was starting to believe.*

Suddenly my phone rang and startled Katy, waking her from her deep sleep. Quickly, I reached for my phone on the night stand.

"Hello," I said into the phone.

"Hey Mike, this is Marx. I have some information I have to share with you. I got this strange letter from a friend with a hot tip. I have no reason to believe it's a trick," he said. "Can I come over?"

"Can you give me an hour?" I asked, not wanting to tell him where I was. "I had to go out for a few minutes and I will be home shortly."

"Good, see you then," Marx said and hung up.

I turned to Katy and immediately I saw her concern, as somehow, she must have known who was on the other end.

"Marx on the phone?" she asked.

"Yeah, he thinks we've got a hot lead and we may need to be making a trip," I said looking away because I knew I had promised to protect her. If I left, it would leave her alone. Alone was not what Katy needed right now.

"Mike, look at me," she said. "I'm going to be okay. I know this is what you have to do. I am worried, but I have learned to be stronger. I can take care of myself.

I just want you to be safe and just remember, Marx is a cop and you're not. You don't have to take the lead."

"I know, I get it, but there is so much that I have left undone and the only way I can find my redemption is to see this to the end with Marx. We're in this too far to back off now."

"Mike, I understand, but I want there to be an 'us.' I've always wanted there to be a you and me. Please, be safe."

"I'll call when I know more, but right now, I have to get home before Marx gets there," I said.

I leaned over and kissed Katy. It was real, just like every kiss had been with Katy, and I hoped there would be more. But I did have to stay alive for that to happen. I dressed quickly and kissed her once more as she walked me to the door. "I'll see you soon," I said.

Katy shut the door behind Mike and leaned her back against it, thinking to herself, *I sure hope so, I sure hope so...*

_▲_

It was eight-thirty in the morning and Andy Marx was at my door. I let him in and offered him some coffee as I had brewed a fresh pot when I got home from Katy's. He took a cup, black, and sat down at the kitchen table. He pulled out the letter he had gotten at work.

"Look, what I am about to tell you is just between you and me. You can't let anyone know and I mean anyone. This note is from Carrianne, I am sure of it. She's not supposed to be contacting anyone while in witness protection," he said looking guilty. "She thinks she has the address of where Jake and Branch are heading. She also wants us to bring in Jake safely. She thinks if we do that, it can help the FBI catch the head of the cartel."

"Wow! I had no idea she would ever be heard from again," I said astonished by this revelation

"What you said a while back about the list of the dead being helpful, well, she is on the list that is dead to us. I never thought we would get this kind of break," Marx said, starting to look like the thoroughbred that was anxious at the starting gate.

"So, when are we leaving?" I asked. "I know you're chomping at the bit."

"We have a few things to check out first, but we have to have our plan, meaning just you and me. We have to be careful not to blow it, but we have to beat them there. By my calculations, we have twenty-four hours to get there ahead of them. Here's what you're going to need to take with you...We began to plan.

CHAPTER 29

B renda Jackson had just gotten up and had showered and was getting ready for work. She had not seen Allison Branch for some time now, but the news of the big explosion and death of two people had her thinking she would hear from her soon. Allison probably needed money, and she would have to find a way to get it to her if she was asked. Breanne, her late sister, would have wanted her to help in any she could. Allison had been Breanne's partner in crime and in life. Brenda knew she would do anything for Branch.

She had just finished getting ready and was gathering up her keys and purse when the phone rang. She knew it must be Branch.

"Hello," Brenda answered.

"Brenda, this is Allison, and I can't stay on long but I want you to do something for me."

"Allison, are you okay?" Brenda asked quickly, interrupting Allison. "You're lucky you weren't killed in the explosion. Where are you?"

"Look, we're heading for Chicago and thought of stopping in Henderson, Kentucky. We need some things, money, clothes, and, most important, good disguises. We can't go to Chicago and get the money as we look now. We must become someone else, and it's very important you contact a person for me. The person works in downtown Chicago and makes silicon masks. He's one of the best. Ask him to do two older people, one man and one woman. You should be able to pick them up today. Bring them to Henderson and bring some money, about five thousand, and I'll pay you back when we get the money in Chicago."

"Are you sure we have time for this?" Brenda asked.

"You have to call this number I'm giving you right now. He owes me this one favor. Write it down. Jake and I are about seven hours away. The man won't tell you his name, just ask for the masks."

Brenda wrote the number down and got her last instructions from Allison. She would have to call in sick today and maybe tomorrow to make this happen.

"Allison, be careful," Brenda said. "This has been all over the news and you know that the FBI is on it."

"Jake and I will worry about the FBI. You just get us the money and the masks. I think my plan will work and then the money will be mine and there is a lot of it. Then we all can disappear. Remember, those masks are the most important things for us to escape. Henderson, Kentucky, is the place and let's say ten hours if all goes well. I can make you very rich for this effort."

Brenda hung up and dialed the number Allison had given her. The man said he had a couple of good masks that she could have that were already made. He reminded Brenda to make sure to take the make-up that goes with them. It was most important for the make-up to blend in with the mask, especially around the eyes and mouth. Brenda wrote down the information and the address where she could pick them up. She called into work sick and, then, made her way to the car. She needed to stop by the bank first and get the money that Allison needed. She paused and thought that maybe this was too complicated and that she may not be able to do this. But Allison had been her friend for a long time. Breanne would have wanted Brenda to help Allison. That driving force made Brenda move and get going. Ten hours to get this done, and Brenda had no time to waste.

──▲──

Henderson, Kentucky, was just a few miles away, and Jake was exhausted. He was glad they were stopping, and he needed rest. They checked in to the hotel and then went directly to the room. They dropped their backpacks on the bed and Jake quickly laid down while Allison went to the bathroom to shower. They were so tired, they barely spoke. Jake drifted into his thoughts and fought sleep even though he knew it was what he needed. He got up off the bed and went to the window. He dared not open it. They were on the third floor and he could see directly across from the hotel to another one across the street.

I wonder what happened to Carrianne. As time had gone by, I was less angry with her and more wishing that I could see her. I miss her and I miss my mother. I hate myself for not making that trip to see my mother before I left South America. I may never see her again, but when this is over, I will try to find her. For most of our time in the states, it was all we had... each other, that was it. Surely, Carrianne could

take me in, right? But it's not going to happen, Jake,
you know that, it just has gone too far and this
woman, Allison Branch has me cornered. I was all in
to help her and I was going to see this to the end.
What is the end, and how is it that she has this magic
over me? Was she leading me to my death? It was
not my brain, not my intuition that was leading me.
It was my heart and my heart will not let Allison
Branch down. She needs me and I need her. Soon,
very soon, we would have the money and we would
leave the states. We will disappear and live the life
that we both deserve. Is she dreaming the same
dream?

Suddenly he felt her touch as she rubbed his back
and moved her hands up to his shoulders and began
to massage them gently.

"Jake, we're almost there. We get the money
tomorrow and all is well," she said as she continued to
rub the back of his neck.

Jake turned to face her and saw that she stood
completely naked in front of him. She was beautiful to
him, and he completely ignored her reconstructed
face. It had not been a factor in how much he had
grown to love her. They get the money and he would
take care of that. Her body was stunning and those
eyes, so blue, so beautiful had grabbed his heart and
he was sure that she loved him, too. He put his arms
around her and held her close to him. He looked into
the eyes that were his weakness. It was not only his
weakness, but it was everyone else's weakness, too...
Parson's, Breanne's, Andres', even Carrianne's. She
had won them over with that one physical feature,
those captivating eyes.

He wanted to make love with her, but he knew that
it could distract from him keeping watch. He was
losing control, and like Andres had said many times

before, he was impetuous and acted too often on impulse. Jake did lose control, and Allison took charge. They made love and lay quietly afterwards, spent and tired, they both fell asleep.

▲

Brenda Jackson was nearing Henderson, Kentucky. She knew she would get there by 3:00 am, but she needed to call Allison and get the address of the hotel. She dialed her number.

Allison jumped when the phone rang and startled Jake awake as well. Jake slowly got out of bed and looked out the window.

"Hello," Allison answered sleepily.

"This is Brenda and I am almost there. I have the disguises with me," she said hurriedly. "They cost me a couple thousand."

"Don't worry, I'll reimburse you with the money," Allison said. "I need you to do one more thing for us. Stop by the all-night People Mart and pick up some clothes older people would wear, things like sweatshirts, jackets, and pants. If we are going to make the disguises work, we need those kinds of clothes. There is one on West Fort Street, just two blocks from us. The address is 2241 East Providence, it's the Sleep Well Inn. It's nothing fancy for sure, but it had to do. You can't miss it. There is the River Inn Hotel across the street on Providence."

"Okay, I should get there in two hours including the stop at People Mart," Brenda responded.

"Okay, we'll see you in a couple of hours."

Allison hung up and tossed the phone on the bed.

"Jake, Brenda is almost here. She is about two hours away. She is bringing the disguises and some clothes we will need. Jake, Jake..."

Startled and looking bewildered, Jake turned from the window and as if not even hearing Allison he got his gun and attached the silencer to it. "I thought I saw something outside just going to check. I'll be back in a few minutes. Until then, you stay out of sight," he said moving quickly. He kissed her on the cheek, and left the room.

Jake moved swiftly as what he saw out the window was what he hoped would not happen. Aberto and Oscar had caught up to them, and he saw them walking from the car to the hotel lobby across the street. He had to act quickly and needed to take them by surprise. There was no time to waste. He hurriedly made it to the River Inn Hotel entrance and watched from outside as they checked in. They had their backs to him as he tried to read the clerk's lips, and he thought he could make out "second floor" as she talked to them and then pointed to the elevator. They both entered the elevator and Jake hurried inside to the stairwell. Undetected, he slipped into the stairwell and ran up to the second floor. Luckily, he was able to see them walking towards him as he waited outside the stairwell door. He watched through the glass as they stopped at their room. He quietly opened the door and snuck up on them. They opened the door to their room and started to go inside.

"Don't move and get your hands up on your head. Do not turn around or you are dead."

Aberto spun at the sound of Jake's voice and Jake shot him in the head. The sound was muffled, and Jake shut the door while still aiming the gun at Oscar Stephenson. Alberto had fallen to the floor, and the blood pooled quickly around his head. He would soon be dead.

"Don't make a sound, my friend," Jake said feeling powerful and in control. He now had his wish to avenge Allison's treatment as a child at the hands of this man. She would never know it happened.

"So, I know who you are, now," Jake said still holding the gun steady on Stephenson. "An animal that treats women and children badly, an abuser. I wish I had the time to torture you for all the things you did to Allison. But really, a person like you is not even worthy of that. You just need to be executed. Drop to your knees."

Jake shot Stephenson twice in the back of the head. No more discussion and no more pleas. Just like that, he had ended the life of Allison Branch's father, and he felt not an ounce of remorse. They would not be found until tomorrow, and he and Allison would be long gone. He calmly and quietly walked to Stephenson's lifeless body and dropped the note that Garon had written intended for Allison, on Stephenson's back.

Now I have redemption for Allison and the way she was treated as a child. Andres would have been proud of what I had just done. It was the right thing to do. They had to be eliminated, it was them or us.

He walked out and quietly shut the door. He headed once again to the stairwell and walked down the flight of stairs to the lobby. He opened the door slightly to check, and then made his way through the lobby and out the front door. Sure, the cops and FBI will see the video, but we will have disguises and they won't find us. All is well... for now.

CHAPTER 30

M arx and I drove to Chicago and arrived about 9:00 am. Marx had been to Chicago many times, and he knew where he was going to set up surveillance. By his estimation, we were where we needed to be and should be ahead of them. Across the street from the address where William Montaldo was waiting, there was a small bakery and coffee shop on the second floor. The front door of Montaldo's place was in plain view and any movements made to enter would be seen. We walked up to the shop and had a coffee and sat by the window overlooking the residence. The street was busy with traffic but the view of the sidewalks in both directions was not obstructed. Marx took out a picture of Jake he had from the last investigations and one of Allison that was the police sketch from Miami. He studied them both. It was now 10:00 am.

"Jake's the protector right now and he's not going to let her go anywhere alone. We'll be dealing with two very dangerous people. If the timing is all good, we should be able to see them enter," Marx said.

"Why don't you call the FBI?" I asked.

Just then, his phone rang.

"Marx here," he said quietly...yeah, uh huh, holy shit! Where?... Ok, keep me posted."

Marx hung up and looked up at me. "More dead bodies."

"Who?"

"That was Chrisler from the FBI, they just got word from authorities in Henderson, Kentucky, that they have two dead at the River Inn. They were on their way to question people at the Sleep Well Inn across the road after receiving a tip about Jake and Branch. The clerk thought a couple that checked in looked like the television sketches of Jake and Allison. They are not in the room. They are going to investigate and hopefully identify the dead bodies."

"So, they could be on their way now," I said, looking out the window. "How far is Henderson from here?"

Marx picked up his phone and googled the distance. "A little over six hours it looks like. They could be here within the next two hours. Depends on when they left."

My skin began to crawl as I knew that this might be that time, when I had to decide. *Could I pull that trigger? Well, could I? She couldn't be too far and yet, once again, I might not even know her. She could be anyone, any stranger on the street. It kept happening over and over, Allison Branch disappearing and reappearing in my life. "Rest assured," my father always told me, "your past will always find you out." Yes, she was my past and now my present. She just could not be my future.*

"Mike... Mike, snap out of it," Marx said in a quiet

but forceful voice.

"I'm okay," I answered, still trying to shake those thoughts from my head.

"Look, you must stay focused. If you're going to stay with me, I need you to be alert and help me out. You can go back if you want, I can handle it if you can't," Marx said with certainty in his voice.

"No, I'm really okay. I was just thinking of something my father had told me some time ago. Really, I'm okay," I said with less certainty than Marx.

"Well, okay. Now, we just sit and wait. You stay here and I'm going to check the streets and alleys around the place. If you see anything suspicious, call my phone. I won't leave the front of the street area, so we won't miss them," Marx said as he got up from the table to leave. "I'll be back soon."

Marx left me sitting there sipping my coffee. I looked at the silent scene of cars and people passing on the sidewalks. Each person that walked by the building, old, young, couples and singles...I thought it could have been them. My eyes were riveted on the scene, not wanting to miss anyone. None of them stopped at the residence.

I saw Marx walk casually across the street, and he stopped to peer down the alleys as he went. I wondered who might be watching him, if anyone at all. As each minute passed, my adrenaline was beginning to spike, my armpits began to sweat. I was feeling clammy and began, once again, to doubt myself. I just couldn't mess this up. The nightmare that was Allison Branch had never left my mind and now she was about to appear again...

_____▲_____

Jake used his key and quietly let himself back in the

room.

"What was out there?" she asked.

"Nothing, really," he said. "Just thought I saw something, but it must have been just shadows."

"You were gone a while, and I was getting worried," she said softly.

She moved towards Jake and put her arms around his neck. He was her man, now. She had someone to believe in that accepted her for what she was. For one of the first times in her life, she felt safe. She absorbed the moment and, for just a brief time, the world went away. The ring of her phone startled her, and she went pick it up.

"Hi, it's Brenda. I'm here in the parking lot. What's your room number?"

"224," Allison replied.

"I'll be up in a minute."

Brenda gathered up all her bags and headed into the lobby. She got on the elevator and proceed to room 224. Allison had watched out the peep hole in the door and saw Brenda's face. She opened the door quietly and let her in.

"It's good to see you," Allison said. "Thanks for helping us out."

Allison then hugged Brenda, and Brenda, seeing Allison's face, was glad she wasn't facing her so that she could compose herself. She had changed since she saw her last and that changed had shocked her. Allison's voice was certainly recognizable, but her face had changed.

"Glad I could be here, too," Brenda said as they held each other's hands, facing each other. Brenda saw her eyes and it was unmistakably Allison. But yet, Allison had changed. Her face was still marred by the scars of the explosion. Brenda had regained her composure and then began to set all the bags of things they needed on the bed.

"Oh, Brenda, this is Jake. I told you about him."

"Nice to meet you," Brenda said staring at him as he was very handsome. She looked away and back to Allison.

"I brought everything you needed. Clothes, the disguises, shoes, and jackets. It should all be there."

"We have to get moving quickly," Jake said and began to take the disguises out of the bag.

"The guy showed me how to do the make-up and I will help you get these on, then get dressed. They look so real, I couldn't believe it!" Brenda exclaimed. "It's amazing!"

"Well, let's get to it," Jake said and with that, Brenda went to work.

About thirty minutes had passed and Brenda was putting the finishing touches on the make-up. Allison and Jake were pleased with their disguises. No one could possibly pick them out in a crowd. Allision stood in front of the mirror. Growing old had never occurred to her. She had always thought that her life was destined to be a short one and her vanity could never see herself being older and having wrinkles. Actually, she liked it, as it covered her scars.

They finished dressing and gathered up the last few things in the bags. Jake had checked the room once more, careful not to leave anything behind. They were ready to go.

"One more thing about the cars, we need to ditch Anastasia's car at the People Mart. It will throw them off enough to give us just enough time. We get in with Brenda, and we'll be her parents. Next, Allison, you need to call William and tell him we're on our way. Give him a time frame and tell him to keep looking around and if something looks fishy, we just set up something different for later. So far, everything is going to plan. It's time to go."

Allison called William and let him know they were leaving and would be in contact during the trip. She also gave him Jake's instructions on what to look for and to call if anything seemed suspicious. William understood and then hung up.

They left the hotel out of the side door and walked to Brenda's car. Jake got in Anastasia's car and Brenda followed Jake. It was a short trip. When they got to the parking lot, Jake put the car in park and looked up at Allison. "Let's go get the money." With that, they got in Brenda's car and Jake locked Anastasia's car and pocketed the keys. They were off to Chicago...

CHAPTER 31

The crime scene was gruesome with blood all over the floor and blood spatter all over the walls. This had been an execution style killing. The scene and its investigation would take some time. There were videos to be seen and prints to be dusted for, but Paul Chrisler knew what he was looking at. There was really no other explanation except that the fugitives they were chasing had made this kill, but which one? Chrisler read the note to his partner, Jenna Holmes, one more time.

Allison,

I really didn't want to have to tell you this, but all along Oscar Stephenson has been working with the cartel. It was never our intention to let you see him. I thought that you deserved to know. But the Boss had talked to Oscar and to keep working with us, he wanted Oscar to kill you.

He's still out there, somewhere with Aberto and the Boss. Their mission is to kill you. I will protect you as much as I can. But Jake, if he finds out, he will go after Stephenson, possibly kill him.

Allison, Oscar Stephenson is your father. Garon

"Looks like the Medina brothers, Garon and Aberto are now out of the way," Chrisler said looking up from the note. "That leaves Jake to be second in charge to the Boss."

"Yeah, looks that way, doesn't it?" Holmes replied, studying the crime scene in front of them. "There's a lot to cover here. Let's give instructions to the team and CSI before we go. We've got to get someone to Chicago. They've got road blocks on the major highways leading to Chicago. I'm not so sure that she didn't kill him."

"I'm not sure, but it I still think it was Jake. He has much to gain here with the Boss, and with Branch," Chrisler replied.

"Yeah, I'm sure Marx is on this as he told me that he was already there. I called state boys in Illinois and they have a team heading there," Chrisler said, making notes on his phone. "Here's a list of things we need, all the front desk interviews, all the video footage we can get, drawings, and sketches. I'm texting this to the lead man. They can email the information to us. For now, we need to head that way."

They hurried to their SUV and put the emergency lights on. They had no time to waste. They sped out of the parking lot and were headed to the Windy City...

------▲------

They went slowly and under the speed limit. They didn't want to draw any attention to themselves. Brenda was driving and Allison sat in the front seat. Jake sat in the back and was making some notes in his head. He looked out the window and thought it funny that he had ended up in this situation, disguised as an old man. *No one would be looking for older people. The disguises are perfect, but the cars, Brenda's car, most importantly, would be spotted by hotel video. Would they put that together? I just hope we gave ourselves enough time. Time, time, everything was about time. Would they have time, or was time running out?*

Allison and Brenda sat quietly for most of the ride. Brenda finally broke the silence.

"Allison, where are you going after we get the money?" she asked.

"I was hoping we could stay with you until we get everything together to leave the states," Allison replied opening her pill bottle, took two, and washed them down with bottled water. "It won't take long and we won't have much time."

Time, there was that word, again, time...

"Well, sure, of course, you can stay with me," Brenda replied.

"Oh shit!" Jake blurted out. "Roadblock ahead. Stay calm and don't be nervous. We're your parents, Brenda, and you are taking us back home to Milwaukee. Stay calm everyone, and don't panic. Brenda you must do the talking. They slowly pulled up to the officer standing in the road.

"License and registration, please," the officer said to Brenda. The line behind them began to get longer. Jake was worried about Allison, that she may panic.

"What happened?" Brenda asked. "I was just trying to get my parents back home from vacation."

"There are fugitives on the loose," the officer said peering into the vehicle and saw the two older people. "You folks will need to be careful out there. Looks like all is in order here, Ms. Jackson. Have a nice day."

Brenda's hands were sweaty as she gripped the steering wheel. She began to drive away slowly, and she was sure they had gotten by the roadblock.

"Hey! Stop!" the officer yelled. Brenda slowed down and stopped. She rolled the window down.

"Yes, sir?" Brenda asked.

"You've got a low, left rear tire. You need to get that fixed," the officer said.

"Yes, sir, I'll pull off at the next exit," Brenda said. "Thank you."

Sweat was pouring down Jake's back as he held the grip of the pistol in his jacket. Allison was near panic mode, and Jake was worried. The car moved slowly ahead, and they were back to the speed limit again.

"We've got to stop at an exit, quickly," Jake said. "We've got to ditch this car. Brenda, your name is known to Parsons and Marx. We won't get far. The sign says five more miles to the next exit. Pull in to that one and head for a motel parking lot. It looks like there are two at the exit. We must steal a car. This car is going to get us caught."

"Sure, sure Jake," Brenda said, knowing her life as she once knew it was now changing forever.

They pulled into the motel parking lot, and Jake got his transponder cloning device, which could intercept the code from the couples' key fob. He got set up with the alternative key he had with him at all times. From Brenda's car, he waited and watched as the young couple got out of their car with their bags and locked their car with the key fob. Jake intercepted the signal and had the code. He programmed his alternative key quickly, and, as the couple disappeared inside the hotel, he walked over slowly and opened the car door. He waved Allison and Brenda to the car and they transported their things to the new vehicle.

"Brenda, go to the other hotel and Allison and I will

follow you. We ditch your car at the other hotel and then we're out of here. Jake and Allison got into the stolen car and the key started it easily. They would be back on the road as soon as they picked Brenda up from the other lot.

Too much time, Jake thought, *wasting too much time*. They needed to hurry...

CHAPTER 32

Margaret was reminiscing and looking at old pictures of Sheila. Margaret remembered her baptism, her kindergarten picture, her graduation picture. She was always a pretty girl, smart, loving, and innocent. She still ached from her loss, and she felt that she would never be the same. Life would never be good again, no matter how much therapy she would receive. The loss had stung then and it stung now. No one will ever understand the tears that a mother sheds for the loss of their child. Even as an adult, Sheila would always remain her child. Now she was gone, just like that, and no one could ever change the heartache she felt every day.

Margaret never hated Mike Parsons. She was only disappointed that they could not make it together. She had hoped for so much more. She would have wanted grandchildren, but that never happened. A grandchild or two would have helped Margaret in these mourning stages. She would have had some of Sheila to remember and to take care of and nurture. But now, all she had were the photos and the painful memories that haunted her every day.

Margaret looked once more at the writings from Sheila's diary. Sheila was tired, sleepy, sick, and needed to sleep that night. She was suspicious and the writing jumped out at Margaret like it always did. Sheila was telling her in some way, that someone made her feel sleepy, tired and sick. Margaret was sure Sheila had been poisoned and she knew by whom.

She wished Mike was here, he could always seem to comfort her, and she needed to talk. She had so many things she wanted to say.

Just then a news flash came over the TV that two men had been shot in Henderson, Kentucky, that morning. The main suspects were fugitives from the FBI and were allegedly involved in the Miami bombing. Margaret went numb as she knew who it must be that they were chasing. It had to be HER, that crazy witch of a woman that was responsible for taking her daughter from her. She had cold chills, even though she had stayed in her bed clothes all morning with old phots strewn all around her. She brushed her gray hair away from her face and tried to wipe away the tears that flowed down her cheeks. She had mixed feelings as she did not understand if her tears were from hurt or anger, or both.

Margaret did know one thing for sure and that was this crazy episode had to end. She needed to talk to Mike soon...

▲

The local police had taken a complaint from a guest at a hotel on the outskirts of Henderson. Their car had been stolen, and they got the plate information from the owners. It was then under investigation. Later in the morning, they got a complaint from a nearby hotel manager that they had an abandoned car in their lot. They ran those plates also and it appeared the vehicle belonged to one Brenda Jackson from Milwaukee, Wisconsin. The officer, running the plates, called them in to state authorities and began taking notes from both the hotel manager and the couple whose car was stolen. But they were way behind the fugitives and, at the time, they had no idea if it would be easy to put this all together. But time had been on the side of the fugitives as they had a long jump on the authorities.

Chrisler and Holmes had just received the carjacking information and had remembered the Jackson girl from the hospital when her sister, Breanne, had been shot and killed. Quickly, her picture had landed on the TV screens across America. Brenda Jackson's life had now changed forever, as she now was included in the list of fugitives as either an accomplice or an unwilling participant.

Chrisler called Marx once more with the new information and the stolen car description. He told Andy to be careful and to understand they had Feds called in to Chicago to help end this thing.

Holmes called the roadblock officer and the officer was embarrassed that he had missed the wanted fugitives. When the description of the abandoned car was given to him, the officer realized they were right there in front of them. He described the two older people in the car he had stopped. They were medium height, possibly in their seventies. He said they did not look remarkable in any way, except for the woman. He noticed her eyes and how clear and blue they were. Holmes took notes as she continued speaking with the roadblock officer.

Marx had his earphones in while talking to Chrisler.

"I'm on the street and out of sight. I've been on surveillance, but no one has shown up yet," Marx said as he kept his eyes on the entrance to the address where William Montaldo was waiting with the money.

"Be really careful as I think they might be near. The time frame is just about right for them to show up. My guys are about ten minutes away," Chrisler said.

"Okay," Marx said. "Let them know I am here and not to shoot me if I have to go in before they get here. Let's stay coordinated and make sure I know who the contact is, so we move in the same directions."

"Got it," he said and was about to finish his call. Instead, Holmes ran over with information from her notes. "Hold on, Marx, I have something else," he said as he looked down at the notes. "From the description of the roadblock officer, they have a third person with them. Her name is Brenda Jackson. I think that was the sister of the girl that you had to shoot at Parson's place on the lake. It looks like the two people with her might be Branch and Jake, but they're dressed as old people possibly looking about 70 plus years old.

Marx froze for just a brief period I noticed as I was watching him from the coffee house window. Something was up and he was talking to someone in his phone through his ear buds and microphone. He had information and it was going to go down. *Should I stay and wait for his call or should I go help? I could mess it up, but Andy would be in danger. I had to help.* I quickly weighed the options, but I felt it best to go down to the street and be there for my partner. I left the coffee shop and headed downstairs.

I got a cup of coffee from the food truck on the sidewalk and kept my eyes on Marx and the house. He was still talking to someone, and then I saw him hang up and put the phone back in his jacket. I started to sweat and all the flashes of what had happened at my lake place, what happened in Miami, and the chase we were on now, was flooding in quick pictures in front of my eyes. I blinked twice and cleared my eyes. I saw an old couple walking down the street and thought to myself, *nothing unusual,* they walked very slowly in front of the address we were watching and then stopped. The man grabbed the woman by the arm and they went to the door and they were going in! *What? This can't be right. Disguised as old people?* I saw Marx then move towards the front entrance and instinctively, I started to cross the street to help.

"Stop right there," the voice said and as I turned, he flashed his FBI credentials. "We've got someone on the way in," the FBI agent said. "You have some ID?" he asked.

I pulled out my driver's license and gave it to him. "Mike Parsons, um yeah, you stay with me and you'll be safe. We have two guys going to enter."

Just then, I saw Marx stop and head back from the house. I was relieved that he did not go in. Instead he walked towards the side alley. *What was going on?* Just then all hell broke loose. It all happened fast. I heard the crash of the window and then gunfire. *Where's Marx?* I heard screeching tires and then one more shot. Geez, I was worried that Marx had been shot, but then I saw him running to the front from the side alley. The FBI agent left me immediately and headed for Marx. Marx was pointing to the alley and talking fast and furious. The man got in his vehicle and sped away.

I went to meet Marx and see what had just taken place.

"The FBI is now in pursuit. Looks like two got away. I couldn't be sure, but I thought it was two women. I got one shot off, but I don't think I hit anyone. It's HER. She and another woman are on the way and I am sure it was Brenda Jackson."

"Damn," I said shaking my head. "

"We have to stay here and talk to the FBI. You know, I sure hope they get them, in a way, I guess. They have done enough damage," Marx said.

"What about Jake?" I asked. Just then, one FBI agent came out of the house. The other stayed with the body and the captive.

"Are you Detective Marx?" he asked.

"Yes, that's me," Marx responded.

"We've got one dead and one cuffed. My partner is inside. The dead guy is disguised as an old man and the detainee is one William Montaldo. We're needing to remove the silicon mask from the dead guy, but we believe it is one Julio Martinez, aka Jake Benson. We want photos for identification and verification. Our guy is on the chase.

Quickly my mind is rushing, Jake dead, Montaldo arrested, Allison Branch on the loose, again. God, I hope they find her...

CHAPTER 33

Katy saw the news as she was getting home from her new job. The scene was eerily reminiscent of the one she went through in Miami. Her stomach was fluttering and she thought she might pass out from the tingling in her head. There was Andy Marx on TV, speaking directly into the camera, telling the audience that a chase was in progress and that the FBI were closing in on Allison Branch and her accomplice, one Brenda Jackson. Andy wasn't just talking to the audience, she thought. He was talking to her, Katy, directly. *Where was Mike? Is Mike okay?* Katy scanned the scene as Marx talked, looking for anyone that looked like Mike. *There he is! Oh, good, he's alive, he's okay. But she could see that he really wasn't. She had seen this look before when they were hostages, not once, but twice!* He looked worried and perplexed. Branch had gotten away again. *Surely the FBI could run her down, right? They would catch her, most assuredly, they had to.*

Katy picked up her phone and called Mike. His phone rang twice and it seemed to startle Mike as she watched him on the screen. He answered quickly and she had to look away from the news flash as it was too surreal to see him in the background talking to her.

"Mike, oh, I'm so glad you're okay. I was hoping that they would end this without incident, but, as always, Branch leaves a wake of destruction in her path and she escapes," she said with a hint of desperation in her voice.

"Look, Katy, she won't get far," he said trying to reassure her, if not himself. "The FBI, Chrisler and Holmes, have been close to capturing her all the way. I wouldn't be surprised if she is not apprehended by the end of the day."

"We can only hope," Katy suggested not really believing her own words.

"Katy, I want you to keep your doors locked and keep your alarm active. We'll be home soon and I'll swing by when I get back," I said, wishing I was already there and not here. "Marx is finishing up, and then we will probably head back to Milwaukee," I said, not knowing what we would really be doing.

"Mike, please, please be safe. I need you to be here, be here with me."

"I'm going to be fine," I said with more reservation than she could possibly know. "I'll be there soon."

Right, be there soon. Mike, you have no idea if what you told Katy is what's going to happen. You know Marx, and we could be gone for days. Marx won't stop until Branch is caught or dead, and more likely, Marx was thinking of the latter, if I was guessing right.

"Mike, let's go. We've got to notify Milwaukee Police and get an APB out on Brenda Jackson and surveil her home. We have to track what we know and get after Branch, the FBI may or may not catch her."

We were driving, back to Milwaukee, I thought, and I tried to digest what all had happened on this day. Marx was on his phone with Milwaukee Police as I continued my thinking.

This dream, this crazy dream called my life, was slowly and daily spinning out of control. No one could have ever expected such an outlandish story. But if there was anyone who could manage such episodes, it was me. I began to wonder how this happened. Where did it start and when did I change from a focused young man to some character in a story I really didn't want to be in? I was caught on a merry-go-round of events that started with everyone turning their back on me. *No, not right. You turned your back on everyone else! It was a free-will choice I made, I turned on Sheila, my parents, friends, my in-laws, and Joanna, walking away from them all. And, of course, Branch...I didn't pick her. I was officially an asshole, not worthy of redemption.* So, here I was left only with three people I could rely on, Marx, Katy, and of course, Margaret. Three people I could not afford to lose... will there ever be redemption for me?

Marx's phone rang ending my self-rant.

"Marx here," he blurted into the phone.

"It's Chrisler, the copters have a bead on her and the driver. Looks like they're heading in the direction of O'Hare," he said.

"Got it," Marx said quickly and jerked the car hard right on to the next street, turning his flashing lights on and he was at high speed immediately. "Hang on, Mike."

With that, we were on the chase again. In the hunt for HER. The evening sun against my window was starting to penetrate my skin, or was it just the idea that I may meet up with HER again. Branch, the reason I was here to begin with, could soon be my target or I could be HER'S. Do you believe in destiny, Mike? Can you pull the trigger? Well, can you?

▲

"Drive, damn it, drive faster!" Allison screamed to Brenda, clutching the handle of the money she was sure that she deserved. Tears were streaking down her face, and her anger was uncontrollable. They had killed her most recent man, Jake. The only man she was beginning to trust in her life. She had escaped out the back, and that bastard, Marx, tried to shoot them. She had grabbed the suitcase full of money and ran. She hated herself for running, but self-preservation was her instinct. It had always been. No meds, no person, no one thing in the world was going to stop her now. She had completely gone over the edge and everything she was thinking of doing was reckless, and, certainly, not smart. Her thinking was nowhere near rational, and she had made up her mind that if this was going to be the end, she would take everyone with her. Allison was now totally lost in her fury. They all painted her as the bad seed, the child gone wrong, and the adult who was more dangerous than anyone would ever believe by just looking at her. She had not only gone over the edge, she had left the universe, tilt-a whirling out into space and all she could feel was hate. Pure, unadulterated hate. For Marx, the FBI, anyone who wanted her to stand in her way, including Mike Parsons. She gripped the handle of the suitcase hard and her knuckles had turned ivory white.

"I don't know if I can keep driving this fast. I've nearly wrecked us twice," Brenda screamed.

"Faster, Brenda!" Branch yelled as the lights from behind were closing in.

Just then a truck pulled out in front of them and Brenda swerved right, missing the truck by inches. The lights behind them were cut off. Their luck had saved them but the copter was still in the air in hot pursuit. Just then Allison remembered the L Train. They could jump on the L in just another block. Allison peeled off her disguise and told Brenda to put it on after they pulled into the alley one block from the L station. Brenda and Allison had traded parts. Allison was now the daughter and Brenda, her mom. There was no time for makeup. They exited quickly and Allison took Brenda by the arm and led her down the street. They looked quite normal as the local police car caught up with Brenda's car in the alley, guns drawn as they inched closer to the vehicle.

"No one inside," the officer said into his mic.

"Damn it," his partner said almost not believing this scene.

"Just keep walking, be calm," Brenda said to Allison hoping she would ease up on the grip on her arm.

"We get to the L, we're in the clear," Allison whispered in a low voice to Brenda.

They made it and Allison used some of their cash to purchase their tickets. They were headed back to the disguise maker. They were going to change one more time and become new people. *One more time, and then maybe, just maybe, they would get away with it. I deserve it. All those people, terrible people, they would all pay before she left the country.*

The train left and Allison looked out the window, her and her mom leaving on the train together. Just like they used to when they made their trips to Chicago. Allison felt safe, now. Her mom was with her... they were headed to the neighborhood of the disguise maker. They were going to be okay... but

Allison, of course, would never be okay again. This was the last time she would feel this way.

CHAPTER 34

The chase was on and we arrived a bit too late. The car had been abandoned near a L train station and I thought we may never find them before they find us. There was just something about her that was slippery like an eel. We had been here, at this very point, before. SHE runs, SHE hides, SHE strikes, and then SHE runs again. Like Ali, she had performed the rope-a dope so many times, never seeming to take the hardest punch, as she bobbed and weaved around us masterfully.

Marx was visibly frustrated and, for the first time, he was showing signs of slowing down and possibly, even giving up. Marx was many things, smart, perceptive, persistent, but he had never been a quitter. He had bested the best in the academy, including her. But, the signs of wear and tear were beginning to show on his beleaguered face. Neither one of us spoke for what appeared to be minutes but actually was only a few seconds.

"Damn it!" Marx uttered through his clenched teeth. "They can't be far. Let's check the last train out and the destination of that train. We have to try and cut them off."

We got to the station and Marx flashed his badge at the ticket attendant.

"Did you see these people buy a ticket here?" Marx asked as he showed the picture of the old lady and Brenda Jackson.

"No, sir, I did not. But you might want to ask the next attendant booth as I just came on," he responded.

Marx rushed to the next booth and asked the same question to a middle-aged woman attending that booth. She did not recall those faces.

"Okay, thank you," Marx responded in monotone. He turned from the booth and his look of determination had returned.

"Let's get going. I know it's a long shot, but we go to the last station and wait. They may want to get as far away from downtown as they can. It's just a hunch, but it's better than doing nothing," Marx said.

"That would be Cermak, McCormick Place," I said.

"Right, c'mon, let's go."

We ran to his car and Marx put the flashing red lights on, and we were off to McCormick Place. We ran lights at every junction and the traffic was hideous. We weaved in and out of the traffic, and the pace was slowed when Marx had to avoid a large moving truck. I was just hoping we weren't too late and were going to the right place...

▲

Allison's hair was matted around her face and she didn't bother to fix it. She was caring less about her appearance. Brenda Jackson was becoming more nervous as she thought surely someone was going to identify them both, and they would spend the rest of their lives in jail. Brenda knew her troubles were now deep, and she was scared. She had remembered Sheila's death, and it made here sad. Sheila was her friend and Sheila's mom, Margaret, was her friend, too. They had been through so many things together growing up and she now felt somehow responsible for even letting Allison Branch into her circle of friends.

"You know I killed her, right?" Allison asked Brenda as if reading Brenda's thoughts. "I drugged her wine. She had no idea that I cared for her, but she wouldn't pay attention to me. It was easy enough and we wiped it all clean. There's no way they can pin that one on me. It was clearly going to be suicide.

Chills ran down Brenda's spine. She had not known that Allison had drugged Sheila's wine that night. She just thought they were cleaning up for Sheila when she went to bed. But now, she was an accomplice of a stone-cold killer, and there was no way out. Allison would kill her if she tried to run now. She had gone too far and even knowing that Sheila was murdered by Branch, she had to play Allison's game and by Allison's rules. Heat flushed into Brenda's cheeks. She wanted to attack Branch but knew that Branch was too dangerous to deal with at this moment.

The train was rolling along and finally came to the last stop at McCormick Place. They got off at the perfect spot and the Mask Maker lived on South Dearborn Street. Very close to where they got off the train...

Marx put on the brakes and screeched to a halt. We

ran up the steps to the train, hoping, wishing we weren't too late. The train rolled into the station and came to a complete stop. The passengers began to exit and I thought of being in some strange cop show on television. The passengers were young, old, in a hurry, and some, not so much.

I scanned the faces looking for Brenda, mainly, as I didn't think I would even recognize Allison. *No match there. No match. No familiar face. Maybe that one is the old lady. Damn, I couldn't remember what she looked like.* This task was daunting as a mass of people and a quick scan revealed not one person that we could identify. Like the puzzle pieces that all looked alike, the faces began to blend into one another. We could never find them in all this mass of humanity.

Marx looked sick, and he walked slowly over to me.

"We missed them, we had to, there was no one there that fit the description," he said, slowly walking down the steps of the station.

At that very moment, two ladies were walking down South Dearborn Street, mostly unnoticed, just an old woman and her friend, daughter, or some caretaker. It was an everyday scene and no one paid any attention to them. They arrived at the address on South Dearborn and knocked on the door. They were let in as Allison had called ahead. Always just one step ahead, like she had some sort of magical powers, she had escaped once more. They were safe... for now...

CHAPTER 35

Carrianne Martinez, still in witness protection, had heard of her brother's death on the news. She sat down on her couch in her new apartment and held her hands to her face and cried. She had so much wanted Jake to turn on them, like she had done. But she knew in her heart that he never would. From the time he was a young boy, as long as she could remember, Jake had been a stubborn boy, always wanting to prove his worth. Carrianne now felt a deep pain and her heart began to melt. He had died for his stubbornness and he would be buried alone, without her and without his mother. There would be no one there.

She went to the window and looked out at the sleepy little neighborhood that she now resided in, tears still streaming down her face. This place was so different from where she grew up, where she and Jake had spent their dangerous and terrifying youth, only to become pawns of a dangerous cartel. She felt that there was no one person she could turn to. Her life all of a sudden had become an empty, bottomless pit. It would take some time for her to get over this, and, quite possibly, she never would.

She closed the curtains and walked slowly back to the couch and sat down next to her new friend that she had met at work. He was a kind and gentle man, just the kind of man she had been looking for all her life. Just when she thought her tears may subside, she broke down again, sobbing, and distraught, thinking her heart would soon break. She would be sitting there until late at night when she would fall asleep, tears still in her eyes. Her new boyfriend would be with her to console her grief.

She woke up an hour later, and began to ache again from the thought of what she had seen on television. She began to try and point a finger at who was at fault. She blamed herself for even tipping Marx off about Jake. Then, she blamed Marx and the FBI for killing him, and then she blamed the Boss for the years of brainwashing he had done to them all... Jake, Garon, Aberto, and even herself. The Boss was such a cruel man, but it was their only way out of poverty, wasn't it? But Carrianne knew, deep in her heart, who was most responsible. Her thinking focused on Branch.

I thought she was trying to protect us. But no, really, she was just using us. Especially Jake, as she teased him constantly. Branch devoured people, one by one, whomever she came in contact with. Evil is too nice of a word to describe her. It was in her eyes, the ones that misled Mike, Jake, Andres, and even herself. Carrianne knew what she should have done long ago, but instead, for Andres, she had pampered and protected Branch. It was what her father, Andres, had wanted. But why oh why could we all not stop her? Branch was always in command. No one would step in her way, although most everyone felt they needed to, but she controlled every last one of them, controlled them with those eyes, those steel blue eyes, that could love you and hate you at the same time. The hate I feel for her right now is real. The only thing I hope for now is that she dies a terrible death, because I know it was Branch that finally got my brother killed. I'll never get to her, but if I have a chance, I'll end her myself. I have never killed anyone before, but if I ever felt like I could, it's exactly what I feel now.

Carrianne came back to reality as she heard the breaking news on television that Allison Branch and her accomplice, Brenda Jackson, were still fugitives of justice. The police had no clues on their whereabouts and didn't have a lot to go on. The manhunt had become large, and it was like they had disappeared into thin air.

If I get the chance, if I just get that one chance, she thought... and she quieted her thoughts and lay her head back down on the chest of her new man. He gave her comfort she had never known, and there was just more thing to tell him, then he would know. She had never felt this safe, but she still had a large hole as her brother was gone.

▲

Once inside the residence, Allison and Brenda were welcomed by the Mask Maker. His home was a plain and simple existence. It was a simple two-bedroom, one bath house that was hidden in a row of plain and simple homes, just like his. He could afford to live elsewhere, but it was his parent's home, and he found it hard to move once he moved back in after their tragic death. They had both been killed by a drunk driver, and he inherited the home soon afterward. He came back and just never left again. The basement area was his workshop and he was paid well, mostly by criminals and sometimes spouses who wanted to disappear. It didn't matter to him as he made sure they never used his name. He could be a very persuasive person and it was how he had survived over the years without detection. Not one of his clients would ever turn on him or give him up to the authorities. He was much too intimidating.

The Mask Maker worked diligently overnight while Allison and Brenda slept. His art was something to behold, and he was making them both into beautiful women. In the morning, he would apply their new masks, make-up and all. They would be walking free in Chicago to the first car rental place they could find. Fake identification was no problem. Allison always carried a couple ID's with her. All she needed to do was fix one of them with a new picture with her new face.

Branch woke from her sleep early at 6:00 am. Allison Branch began, once again, to feel that strange spirit running through her veins. The one that made her want to kill. She had been through a lot in her childhood, her adulthood, and now in her bid for survival. The blood filling her veins began to warm as she thought of all the things she was going to do. The things that would allow her to avenge everyone that had ruined her life.

Of course, it was everyone else's fault. This life had been torture, thanks to an abusive father, boyfriends that left me, and friends that always shunned me or were taken from me. Never married, never having children, my life was such an empty vessel. The only thing left was the one joy I could now feel, and that was the joy of revenge. I have to have it, and I will have it!

She drew her knees to her chest as she was now sitting up in her bed, Brenda still asleep next to her. Branch dropped her head to her knees. Curled up in her own crazy kind of upright cocoon, she tilted her head back and her thoughts were so crazy and so angry that she dug her fingernails into her calves and scratched hard, drawing blood.

I will kill again. There are only three left. That dumbass barmaid, Katy, Marx, and of course, that shallow man, Mike Parsons, that had not chosen me. I will leave this country and finally have the life I had so much wanted. Yes, I will, but first, they must be dead, all three. They will all pay for what they have made me. They are all going to die...

A loud growl startled Brenda awake. She sat up quickly in bed only to see Allison in her weird cocoon, rocking back and forth. Brenda noticed the blood on Allison's legs and touched her on the shoulder.

"Allison... Allison please stop! You're bleeding, look at your legs," Brenda said urgently.

Allison only mumbled in response. Brenda could not make it out, but, finally, she had brought Allison back to reality.

"Let's clean up those scratches. You must have been dreaming,"

"Yeah... yeah, I guess so," Allison responded meekly as she appeared so worn and tired.

Brenda helped her out of bed and led her to the bathroom. She cleaned Allison's mark and scratches. This was not what she had expected. Brenda only wanted to help her, and now, she had become caretaker and accomplice at the same time. She was in so deep that she may never get out of this horror story.

Brenda led Allison back to the bedroom and helped

her dress. Allison was coming back to reality now and she seemed much better.

She brushed Brenda's hair from her face and looked into Brenda's eyes directly.

"You've been such a good friend. Thanks for helping me," Branch said directing her steel blue eyes directly at Brenda's.

Brenda didn't know how to respond as she felt hypnotized by this strange phenomenon that were Branch's eyes. Piercing, bright and shiny, those eyes held her attention.

"The masks are ready," the Mask Maker said from outside the bedroom door, startling them both. "Get dressed and I will apply them for you."

The girls finished dressing and went downstairs with the Mask Maker to his office. He began his work, taking his time to perfect the make-up of each. He was proud of his work, and they could see in him an artist, painting the picture he wanted to paint. He finished his work and then said, "Before you pay me, take a look. I only do what my clients ask for."

They went to the full-length mirror and they were amazed.

"My god!" Allison exclaimed. "The job could not have been done better. It's so beautiful."

Brenda looked at her own image and was stunned. *This man, this Mask Maker, he was a genius. Disguised like this, I may make it out of this nightmare... unless... unless Branch killed me first.*

Branch went to get her money and the Mask Maker was paid his handsome fee. The women were ready to leave and begin the journey, and they had no idea of how it would end. They only knew it was their only choice, and they had no other options. All they could shoot for now was freedom, and if Allison listened to Brenda, they could get through this thing and be out of the country. But, Brenda, fearing the worst, knew that Branch would have to kill to have her spirit set free. If only Brenda could get her to drop the revenge idea. If only...

CHAPTER 36

Marx and I had barely missed them. We had no idea that we were close, but yet oh so far away. The frustration of Marx was beginning to take its toll. I don't think I had ever seen him quite like this. His eyes were darting all around, looking for a small glimpse of the two figures. There were so many that I knew we would never be able to pick them out.

Marx called Chrisler at the FBI to see if they had anything.

"Hello, Chrisler here."

"Paul, this is Andy Marx. Have you got anything to go on?" he asked.

"No, unfortunately, it looks like they disappeared in thin air," Chrisler replied.

"Damn it, they couldn't have gotten far. They have to be around here somewhere," Marx said.

"I've only got a couple of men to spare, but I'll send them to the neighborhood. I'll have my guys set up the radius near the train station. Maybe they ducked in somewhere. Be careful of any hostage situation like we had in Miami," Chrisler said.

"Okay, got it. We're going to start checking around. Have your guys call me when they are close. We're on South Dearborn," Marx replied and hung up.

He looked at me, tired, angry, but still ready to keep up the chase. "Let's go."

And with that, we started down Dearborn, going door to door and warning the neighborhood to be on the lookout. The news was all over it, too, and when Marx flashed his badge, most of the people knew what it was about.

Most people had seen nothing, and we saw nothing irregular about the people who answered the doors. None of them seemed to be under stress except for the few that thought there was some possibility that they were nearby.

We got through a half dozen homes before Chrisler's guys from the FBI contacted Andy. They made a quick map of the area and the local officers had now joined the hunt. We continued on our row and the FBI went two blocks east and the locals went two blocks west. We had an area, but it might be for nothing. But it was seriously all we had to go on. We had gotten lucky before, maybe we would again.

The Mask Maker looked out the window and saw two men heading towards his home.

"Quick, you two, go downstairs to the shop. I think we have some trouble coming our way. There's a closet down there. Get in there and keep quiet." Allison and Brenda went down the stairs quickly, moving quietly to not make noise. They hid in silence as they heard the knock on the door.

They had been to several homes and had no luck at all. The sixth home was a two-story brick with steps leading up to the front porch door. Marx and I walked up the steps and knocked on the door. The man answering the door was middle-aged with glasses and a receding hairline. He looked like any other average Joe on the block.

"Can I help you gentlemen?" he asked as he stood in the doorway.

"Yes," Marx flashed his badge at the man. "We're looking for these two women" as he showed the man the pictures of Brenda and Allison. "They are extremely dangerous and have been running from the police and FBI for the past several hours. We have reason to believe they may be in the area."

"Well, I haven't been out and about much today," he replied. "When I was out to get the mail, I didn't see anyone."

"If you do see anyone that fits this description, contact the local police, or you can call me at this number," Marx said as he handed him his card.

The man looked at the card for more than a few seconds. "Detective Marx, Milwaukee Police Department... hmm... okay Detective and thanks for the heads up," the man said looking distracted for a moment.

We walked back down the steps and continued on our way down the block. Marx was pensive, and I could tell something was bothering him. We checked several more houses and met up with the FBI men that Chrisler had sent. They also had no luck. Another Allison Branch dead end.

———▲———

The Mask Maker quickly went down to the shop and opened the closet door. The two women walked out nervously, looking around for others in the house.

They were sweating behind their new masks and they were glad to get out of the dark closet. With Allison's condition, Brenda was glad to be out of there, too. She feared that in that closet, Branch could lose it without warning.

"Don't worry, they are gone now. You two need to get away from here, and soon. I'm worried that you will be seen and I didn't like the look of the one cop. Somehow, I think he had, in some way, knew or sensed you were here. He might be back."

"It's Marx," Allison said. "Was there another man with him?" she asked.

"Yes, but funny thing, he never produced a badge," the Mask Maker said.

"Parsons," she said immediately.

Brenda flinched at the names. She knew how this would set Allison off into a rage. She immediately went to Branch and touched her arm lightly.

"We just have to worry about getting out of here, and soon. We don't have time to go off the deep end. Allison... Allison! Brenda saw it in her eyes immediately. She was in that mode, the mode that she had seen before when Mike Parson's name had come up. Deep and distant, her eyes were burning a hole into something. It was something in her mind, in her imagination, that kept her focused on the wall in front of her.

"Allison... we've got to go. They may be back and we need to be gone," Brenda said.

Allison came back to reality, shaking her head from side to side as if awakening from another one of her bad dreams. She could not think or focus on anything except the flash back to the bar, when Mike Parsons moved to the bar from her table to that other bimbo. *All of this, this craziness, HE created it all. He didn't pick me. Do you believe in destiny, Mike? Well, do you?*

They had reached the top of the stairs, Brenda holding onto Allison's arm, supporting her all the way up the stairs. She stopped and Allison seemed to come out of her self-induced fog, looking at Brenda with a look that Brenda knew was bad.

"Call us a cab," Brenda said to the Mask Maker. It was a risk, but they needed out of there right now. Brenda sat Allison down in a chair and quickly went to get the money. The cab would be here soon, and they had no time to waste. Allison had started to come back to reality and, slowly, her fog had begun to recede. Brenda was worried that they wouldn't survive Marx, Parsons, and the FBI, but she was more worried they may not survive Allison's mental condition.

The cab pulled up outside and soon, they would be off, and Brenda had to take control of where they were going. Allison was becoming incapable of anything rational. Brenda had a lot of challenges in her life and controlling her little sister had been one of them. Breanne was dead now and somehow it was related to Brenda's inability to protect her like she should have. The pain came back to her instantly. She had lived with the thought of letting her mother down and not delivering Breanne from the fate of death. Now, she had to keep Branch from the same fate. It would be her biggest challenge, and she just couldn't fail.

The Mask Maker opened the door and asked Brenda, "Where will you go?"

Allison broke in and spoke for Brenda. "We're going to Downers Grove. My mother's there waiting."

Brenda began to speak and then thought better of it. "Okay, sure. We'll go to Downers Grove."

With that, they headed down the sidewalk and Brenda thought that somehow, she had to find a place to go, and in her mind, it wasn't going to be Downers

Grove. Brenda could not have possibly conceived what was going to happen next, but then again, she was the sane one...

CHAPTER 37

The Chemist had boarded the plane at the front of the line. He appeared to be coming to an end in his long journey back into anonymity. He had made it from Atlanta to the east coast and now was ready to fly back to France, a place where he could hide for the rest of his life. He had accomplished much and had all the wealth he needed now.

The only person to worry about now was the Boss. He had been loyal, that is, up until now. The Boss had provided him with many opportunities to use his skills for a fortune of money. The Chemist was tired and actually felt that he was done killing and that there had to be some other life where he could try to learn to enjoy what was left. He just had to get to France to make it happen. He wondered to himself if it would ever be possible to have any other kind of life than the life he knew.

He was seated comfortably in his seat and started to read on his phone. He looked up and a cold chill worked its way up his spine, as the person he most feared just walked on the plane. The Boss seemed to be searching and looking and then, their eyes met, cold, heartless and menacing, they both just stared. Two men, that had made life a brutal journey for pay, had finally come to a moment where it would be do or die. Jeremy Todd had his life flash before him before, but this time, it was more intense. The Boss had found him and nobody finds Jeremy Todd, The Chemist. The Chemist felt the need to recall his dead sergeant's mantra of "kill or be killed." It would dive him in the next thirty minutes. The longest or last hours or minutes in his life... he had no way of knowing which it would be...

The Chemist kept his eye on The Boss. *He found me, but how? I had always been the best at not being detected. He can't be that good, or can he? I only have this flight time to kill him, before he kills me. But neither one of us can do that. Too many witnesses are on this flight. Something had to happen before they landed in France, or, Jeremy Todd would meet his demise. Jeremy had an idea, and it had to work.*

The Chemist had with him a pill, one he would take if he was ever caught and interrogated. The pill was for use in the military in special services. It was a suicide pill. He thought if he could just get near the boss's drink, he could slip it in his coffee. It was his only chance and the Boss may never leave his seat. If only he would get up to use the bathroom.

As luck would have it, the Boss did get up and go the restroom. *Move now, Jeremy. You don't have much time.*

He quickly moved near the Boss's seat and the woman on the inside window seat smiled at him politely.

"Nice view from your window, isn't it?"

"Yes," she replied looking out the window and the Chemist quickly dropped the pill in the Boss's coffee.

"Have a great flight, ma'am," he said and then moved up to talk to one of the stewardesses. He returned to his seat before the Boss could get back from the restroom. There would be an emergency on the plane very soon. Jeremy Todd would be free again, slipping away into the darkness of anonymity once more. It is where he most wanted to be, unnoticed and incognito.

He didn't move when the Boss went into convulsions near the time they were about to land. The passengers on the plane had rushed to help the man who appeared to be having a heart attack. The lady sitting next to the convulsing Boss was terrified. Jeremy kept his cool and hardly moved. The plane landed and an ambulance was dispatched to the aircraft. They would be too late and Jeremy knew this to be true. The Boss would be dead before they got there. The passengers would be allowed to exit the plane and the Boss would soon be on the way to a morgue. E-4 Specialist Jeremy Todd had completed his last mission and the Boss would never be a problem to him again.

He exited the plane and walked away as he had done so often. Whether it was luck or skill, or a combination of both, Jeremy Todd, The Chemist, had walked away again to once more slip into his private and dark world. He had done many things that he regretted but did out of a sense of duty. But, he knew he had killed for money too, and probably not for the last time. It was how he made his living, and now, and possibly forever, he would escape to a much quieter kind of life. For at least a time, he would stay hidden. That was just fine with him.

▲

The Mask Maker had once again had a very handsome payday. He had done so many of these, it had hooked him, and he was addicted to making criminals disappear. He had done it so often and now he needed a quick vacation, and he was getting out of Chicago as fast as he could. He packed up his things and was heading for the front door. He rolled the suitcase and stopped to go get his car keys. When he returned to walk out of the door, there was a knock. He opened the door and Marx, in his bold way, was already in interrogation mode. Marx had the gut feeling that this man was not being truthful and that something was not quite right.

"No more playing games. You know where they are and where they are going!" he yelled

"I don't know what you are talking about," he said with a frightened look.

"Yeah, you do. Now tell me," Marx said as he pointed his drawn pistol at the mask Maker.

"Don't shoot me, please. They came here for help. I made their disguises. They paid me well."

"You aided fugitives and I am placing you under arrest. If you don't want to spend real hard time, you better let me know where they are going," Marx said almost demanding the answer.

"Downers Grove, they said something about Downers Grove and being close to her mother," The Mask Maker said shaking a bit from Marx's aggressiveness.

"You better be right. If not, I'm coming back for you, and won't be to arrest you," Marx said and holstered his gun and motioned for me to get going. "We are going to Downers Grove." What the hell does SHE mean about her mother being there? She's been dead for a long time. Allison must be worse than we thought. We don't have much time and it is getting near sunset. It will be dark when we arrive at Downers Grove, in more ways than one..."

CHAPTER 38

Marx and I left the Mask Maker's house and got into Marx's vehicle. As I closed the car door, my phone buzzed in my pocket. When I looked at Caller ID, I saw that Margaret was on the line. I had to answer because what if Margaret needed me.

"Mike, this is Margaret. How are you doing?" she asked. Are you okay?" Are you safe?" she asked

"Look, we are going to be fine." I said, not really believing myself at the time. Marx's voice was a bit louder in the background and I wished he would keep it down a bit.

"Where do you think she is headed? Is she coming back to this area?" Margaret asked me.

"I don't know yet, but when we are done with this mission, I will call you," I said, wanting to keep Margaret out of this at all costs.

Marx's car was roaring by now and headed towards interstate 290 and we would get on to West Ogden

Avenue. Once we hit West Ogden, we would have an hour to travel. Then, if we could find them, life could get really crazy.

"Margaret, be safe and keep your doors locked, just in case," I said.

"We're headed to Downers Grove!" Marx exclaimed loudly into his phone while talking to the FBI. I told her that I had to go and that we needed to get moving because everything was about to get crazy. I said goodbye and hung up the phone.

I put Margaret out of my mind and focused on what would now be our newest game. It would be a guessing game and that was about all we could do... guess.

Marx drove in silence as the flashing light on top of his vehicle blinked incessantly. I kept my thoughts to myself.

We had talked about this case over and over many times. We had been through many things, including our near deaths and the deaths of other sordid characters in this mess. We had been through so much that you could say we were like two totally different men, two totally different stories, but each seeking something to redeem us, to make us heal from something we could never really put our finger on. Each of us so different and yet each of us still quite the same.

I was feeling, at this moment, that I was now in the final stage of what would either be my living or dying redemption. The road on this journey had taken me many places, but it never seemed to really deliver me anywhere that I had wished it would. I kept asking for something that just wasn't there. Every time I knocked on the door, it never opened. It just left me standing there. Every now and then, the door would open just a crack to let me see a glimpse of what it was that I was asking for, only to slam shut once more. I began to think that in my life, it was just a cruel joke, this theory of being able to redeem yourself. It had gotten to the point of frustration and self-loathing, thinking I didn't deserve much better than what I got. The idea of finally settling into a life like most normal people had, like kids, grandkids, silver and golden anniversaries, they were something that would never happen to me. I wondered to myself, if in reality, those friends of mine were really happy or were we fooled by all that we were told when we were kids and that we could live the exact same lives that our parents did? Watching all my friends live that life, were they happy? Lessons learned in life by our parents sometimes weren't passed on to children because the lessons learned were just too embarrassing or too difficult to recall.

The lessons learned were choices and they were done. They were in the past and there was no changing that. Like most self-help gurus would say, "you move on, you go forward, but when I moved forward one step, the heavy burden of my past kept me feeling like a pack mule just trudging along at such a slow pace. Maybe that was it, I didn't have the patience that the pack mule had. I wanted this redemption thing to come fast. But how could you make something happen so fast that took years to bring down. There were many miles to go and the pack mule just had to keep going. I just wanted to be the racehorse. Being the winning thoroughbred at the Derby was what I wanted. But life just turned me into the pack mule, trudging along, carrying those heavy burdens of a life not necessarily well-lived.

I finally escaped my thoughts and saw the sign that said Downers Grove ten miles. We were almost there.

I had hoped all along that we were right and the Mask Maker was telling us the truth. It just couldn't be a wild goose chase anymore. This had to end, the pack mule carrying the heavy load. This pack mule was getting very tired...

CHAPTER 39

Katy was more worried about Mike now than she had ever been. She had not heard from him for the past few days, and she knew he was in this chase with Marx. Her thoughts kept going back to the kidnappings, the pain and suffering, and the pure evil that existed in the heart of Allison Branch. She had just gotten home from work, and she was pacing the living room floor and the news had covered this story for a while now. She just had no idea where he was, and she was wishing he would call.

She had wondered if she had overstepped her limits with Mike and if he was going to be serious about her. She didn't want to doubt him, and she had desperately wanted him to be with her for such a long time.

It just had to be this time, right? I have had it so bad for him for so long. I know him better than anyone and I think he knows that. Who knows you better than your bartender? But I was more than his bartender, wasn't I? What if he doesn't come back this time and the next time I see him is in the morgue? This just has to end, and he has to come back.

Katy came back into reality and she found herself staring out her deck's sliding glass door. It was getting on towards evening, and she could see the sun lowering itself on the horizon. She saw the sun getting caught behind a tree that was not fully in bloom. The tree looked old and beaten for some reason. She tried to peer through the late afternoon haze and the yellow-gold light shining through the tree. It was giving her hope that even though it was in an early stage of spring, the tree would soon bloom. It gave her hope that her relationship with Mike would grow and prosper like that spring tree.

It could happen, it really could. I am sure of it.

Katy could not sit still and began to pace again with her thoughts. Alone with her thoughts again.

He just had to some back. Where is he?

⸻▲⸻

Brenda Jackson was in a panic. She had driven Allison to this place called Downers Grove. She had heard of it before, but this was her first journey here and she wondered what in the hell she was doing here. The cops had to be smart enough to be on their trail and here they sat at an arboretum parking lot. People were leaving and they were hardly noticed at all.

"Look, Allison, we don't have to stay here. This is so close, and do have enough of a head start to make a change," she said looking at Allison and shaking her head yes, hoping to get her approval.

"She's here, you know. My mother, she is here. She's been waiting for me for a while," Allison said looking skyward. "This where we went together when

I was little. We came here because of the trees. They were always pretty, and, oh, the one by the pond, that was my favorite. I used to climb up in that tree and watch the ducks swim on the pond."

"Allison, listen, at least let me drive you and around and think about this. There are just too many people here, and we will be noticed by someone. I know we look different but if someone notices we have masks on, they may think something funny. C'mon, it makes sense, right?"

"I want to be here! It's what I feel, that we'll be safe here," Allison said, almost too tersely for Brenda's liking.

"Just a ride, right, we can come back if you like. It's just too light outside to sit here," Brenda pleaded.

Allison hesitated just a bit, and, although she could not read her face, Brenda could see her eyes and she saw that maybe, just maybe, Allison would be okay with this idea.

"Maybe you are right," Allison said. "But, just for a while, you have to promise me that we will come back here. I just need to see this place one more time. I know I can recover, if I can just see her one more time. I will be better when I see mom."

Brenda was relieved, and she had no intention of coming back here. They were going to get further and further away from this place. Then they would get a plane and get the hell out of the states. Brenda had an idea and she was going to convince Allison that there was a better way out of this situation. Allison had gone over the edge and Brenda had recognized that if they had any chance of getting out alive, they had to make a run for it, not stay in this town. Brenda knew that she was the only one that could make that happen.

Brenda put the car in drive and slowly made her way through the parking lot and drove. The further away she got, the better she felt. It was getting easier and Brenda found a nice county road and began to glide down the road. She rolled the window down as she wanted the cool spring breeze to hit her face. Her trying to convince Allison to leave the arboretum had worn her out and her blood pressure was rising, as she could feel that heat in her cheeks. She was beginning to feel better. It would only last for a while...

▲

Andy Marx and I had arrived in Downers Grove and had immediately gone to the place he thought she might be. The parking lot was empty and there were no more cars. We were the only ones there and the parking lot lights were shining dimly in the early evening darkness. It was evident she was not here.

So, this is where this had all led me. To a dimly lit parking lot in an arboretum in Downers Grove, Illinois. I should laugh to myself, right? This is funny. All the emptiness that is inside is not letting me go and here it is again, just emptiness. I had gone many places with Marx, chasing this woman and to think she is going to end up here. Being all the way down in Miami and here we think she will be here, just a couple of hours from where it all started. It seemed foolish, but yet again, it seemed to make sense at the same time. In some ways, I feel sorry for her and in some ways, I hate her. These mixed feelings were causing me concerns. Could I pull the trigger?... well, could I?

"She'll be here," Marx said assuredly. "There's no way she misses this spot before she makes her getaway."

"I'm not that sure," I responded. "I think if she was smart, she heads out of the country at the first opportunity."

"You don't understand. She always talked about her mom and her going here. She saw the department shrink about it," Marx said flatly, not even blinking.

"What are you talking about?" I asked.

"Her mom... I don't know when she told you her mom died. But it was some time ago. Long time ago." Marx said staring out the window. "They almost fired her over her bizarre behavior, but I talked them out of it. I guess I just felt sorry for her. But it was a scar she carried for a long time."

I wasn't shocked but still knew that I had been fooled by her. Once again, another lie, in the endless pursuit of her crazy, narcissistic dreams, I was someone she wanted to kill, not love. But she set me up so well, and to this day, I can't tell you exactly why I was in love with her. But for sure there was one thing that gave her the control that she needed... those eyes, and it wasn't just me. Jake, Carrianne, Andres, Breanne, Brenda, even Sheila, had that very same experience. How many of them were still alive to even tell their story? Well, Brenda, Carrianne, and I were alive, but how many more would have to die? Would I be one of them? Would Marx? And why had Marx seemed to escape her clutches? He didn't seem to be taken in my her and those steel, blue eyes. He seemed to have this super-power that the rest of us did not have, his resistance to Allison Branch. But why? I couldn't figure it out, but there was a lot about Andy Marx I never figured out. But he was my friend, and I trusted him.

"We wait and see if someone comes in from the street," Marx said. "I have that gut feeling."

When Andy Marx had a gut feeling, I didn't argue.

CHAPTER 40

B renda had thought she accomplished what she set out to do and that was to get Allison Branch far away from the arboretum. She was working up the courage to suggest never going back to the arboretum and they head out. They had the money and what they needed to survive. Brenda could see years of jail time ahead, and there was no other way out but to run.

"Allison, let's leave. We can get a flight out if we go back to Chicago. They'd never look for us there. Surely, they don't think we would go back there. Please?" Brenda pleaded.

"I'm going back, and you're going to take me there!" Allison exclaimed.

"But Allison..."

"No!" she yelled as she pulled her gun on Brenda. "You will take me back, or I will end up going back myself. You do understand, right?"

"No, I can't. Why don't you want to get out when

you can? It makes more sense than you staying around and getting caught."

"You **will** drive me there and right now!"

Brenda could see that she had no choice anymore. She was in for a penny and in for a pound. With the gun pointed at her head, Brenda turned around and headed back.

"You will drive me there and when we get there, don't use the main entrance. I'm sure that Marx will have that covered. I know how he thinks," Allison said while still pointing the gun at Brenda.

"You can quit pointing that gun at my head now," Brenda said as she was now shaking. Allison lowered the gun but kept it ready in case Brenda made a mad dash.

"Pull over here," Allison said. "You can park it and keep the keys. We can walk across the field and sneak into the arboretum. I just need to see my mom before we leave. Security won't see us. I need to see the tree, the one I used to climb as a little girl."

"We don't have to do this. Let's go back to the car. We still have time."

"I said, we go!" Allison said a bit too loud for Brenda's liking, pointing her gun again at Brenda. "We have to be quiet going across the field and stay low. We'll be there in about ten minutes. Now, stay with me, Brenda, and if you make any noise, you're dead."

Brenda just nodded. She was going on a journey that was absolute insanity. She knew it all along. She was just wishing that she could change this scene. She was trapped and now, whatever happened, she hoped she would live through it.

___▲___

Mike and Marx were parked when they got a call from the FBI. Chrisler had a make on the vehicle driven by Branch and Brenda Jackson. It was found in a field near here. Marx hung up and looked over at me. "That was Chrisler. They got the vehicle, and there is an open field leading to the arboretum. We're going in and we must split up or we may not find them. I need you on the side by the pond," he said as drew a map on paper for me. "You'll see it about a quarter mile down that path over there. We hop the fence and go our separate ways. I'll be on the other side of the pond. If you must shoot, do your best. This situation is fluid and you may have to do it, you know, shoot. Don't forget everything I told you. Let's go."

With that, we hopped the fence and quietly went in different directions. I headed down the path had drawn for me. *I could trust him, right? Marx knew this place, right?* I was asking myself these questions as I went down the path. In my mind, it would either be the path to destruction or the path to redemption. I really didn't know my chances as to which it might be.

I noticed every shadow and every movement. I passed some carved displays that made me jump. I didn't know what to expect, but I kept my gun drawn and searched the darkness for HER. Yes, if SHE was here, SHE would be in the shadows, jumping out like a scene in the movies, and shoot me on the spot. My steps were slow and cautious. My whole body felt like a lead weight and to move seemed like a conscious effort, with each step bringing something new to my senses. Everything I saw was HER. Everything I heard was HER. Everything I smelled was HER. My senses were full of HER, and I didn't want HER to take my life from me. I was as ready for this confrontation as I would ever be. I kept walking slowly.

▲

There were lights on the arboretum displays, and Allison and Brenda avoided any light as much as possible. Allison knew they were getting closer to her tree, the one she loved by the pond. A figure, hidden in the shadows, froze as it heard their footsteps coming. Behind a large tree, a figure watched as Brenda and Allison made their way down the path. The figure made sure the two had cleared the brush and was in sight before slowly and quietly following after them. They had no idea that someone was following them.

Allison and Brenda had finally reached the tree that Allison so loved as a little girl. She closed her eyes for just a second and tried to feel her mom there. Her presence always had a calming effect on her, and she looked skyward as a few tears began to slowly fall down her cheeks. It was dark here, but the near full moon had illuminated their faces with a light that had shone on them through the trees. The figure hiding behind the nearby tree had followed them but was confused. These were not the people expected to be here. These people, two women, were not recognizable. The figure kept looking and saw one of them pull off what looked to be a rubber mask. The figure immediately knew they were in the right place.

"She's here, you know," Allison said softly. "She would always bring me here, a place that was just for the two of us. A place where we could hide from my dad. I felt safe here, I always did."

"We can't stay here long, Allison," Brenda said. "Please, let's leave. We can get out while we can."

"You don't understand," Allison said as she moved to sit down against the tree she loved. "It was here that I could be a little girl. Every other place and time in my life, I had to be strong, tough, better than anyone at everything. Here, I could rest and take away the person I had become. I came here to change back to the little girl. Then, I would go back to my life of lies, deceit, and evil, the life I could never shake."

The figure watched as the two continued to talk and knew the voice and face of one of the women. The other was still hard to make out but had to assume it was the crazy one. The figure stayed quiet, still waiting for the time to be right.

▲

I heard voices. They were light, yet not that distant. I should almost be there. I took a few more steps and there it was, the pond, with a moon shining a bright light across the water. I moved slowly towards the voices, along the path, and in the shadows. I could make out two figures and I assumed it was Brenda and Allison, but the closer I got, I was not sure. I could certainly make out Brenda, but Allison still had her disguise on, the face I could not recognize, but the voice I began to make out was certainly that of Detective Allison Branch. I drew my gun and walked closer. If I moved out of the shadows now, I would be seen. *Could you pull that trigger, Mike, well, could you?*

Marx had made it to the back side of the pond and he, too, had heard the voices that were becoming more audible as he moved closer. The weeds around the pond were high enough to hide him, but he had to move slow. He knew this was it, his last job on the force and he wasn't going to fail. Marx could feel it, he had that kind of sense. He knew that soon, something was about to break loose and it would be now or never, do or die. He had to beat Allison Branch just one last time. He drew his service pistol and moved slowly through the high weeds...

CHAPTER 41

"I told you I killed that girl, his ex, Sheila, didn't I?" Allison asked.

I thought it was time. There was no better place in the conversation to jump in. I emerged from the shadows and pointed my gun at the face that wasn't Branch's. She slowly stood and said, "Well, hello Mikey, so glad to see you. See I didn't really kill Sheila, you did. She would be alive today had you picked me."

She slowly peeled the mask off her face, and the moonlight was bright enough for me to see her face. It had been somewhat disfigured from her last injury and the damage was noticeable. She was no longer the pretty woman I had encountered in the Milwaukee Police Department some time back.

I should have pulled the trigger right there, but something in me couldn't.

Go ahead, shoot, Mike!" she yelled and now stood in front of me with Brenda Jackson next to her. "I know, you can't, can you? See, you're not strong like me, you're weak."

"You don't have to do this, Allison. You can put the gun down and save yourself. Marx is coming and the FBI will be here soon. There really is now way out."

"Sure, there is, Mike. There's always a way out. It has always worked that way for me. You know that, I know that. It's that destiny thing. I kill you and Marx is late and won't make it. Brenda and I leave, and I get to do what I want to."

"But your mom, she's watching you, and it's not what she wants for you," I said stalling for time and still pointing the gun at Allison.

"Leave my mother out of this! You didn't know her. You have nothing to say about my mother. I killed your ex. She was getting in the way, of what I wanted. A little poison in the wine was all it took. All my friends liked her, even more than me. You didn't pick me and neither did she. Now, it's time to kill you, too!"

My finger was frozen on the trigger and at that moment, I knew the answer to the question, "*Can you pull that trigger, well, could you?*" And, the answer was no. I just couldn't. I guess I did believe in destiny. I was going to die here.

"I knew you couldn't do it. You don't have the guts. You're that guy that's going to fix everything, well, why couldn't you fix me? Why didn't you try? Tell me that. Why? I wanted you so badly and you didn't want me. Now, I wouldn't take you if you were the last man on earth. Ha! I knew it, you won't shoot me!"

"But I will."

The voice came from the left of Allison, and she whirled to face it. To her shock and surprise, there stood Margaret with a gun pointed at Allison.

It all happened faster than my eyes could see it.

Allison and Margaret both fired, and Brenda instinctively jumped in front of the bullet intended for Margaret. The next shot came, from the pond and it hit the mark squarely, driving the target, Allison Branch, back against the tree she had loved as a child. She slid slowly down the tree and ended up in a sitting position, looking upward as if now, she was finally free. I could feel nothing. What had just happened?

Marx ran up on the scene and kicked the gun away from Allison's reach. He felt for her pulse and there was none. Allison Branch was gone. Her demons and devils now free from her mind, she could no longer be in pain. Marx stayed on one knee for a while, then rose to check Brenda Jackson. He applied pressure to the wound Brenda had sustained to protect Margaret. Margaret knelt by Brenda and grabbed her hand. I looked down and saw smoke coming from the barrel of my gun. *I didn't think I fired. But it all happened so fast.*

"Call 911 and get an ambulance here, quick!" Marx barked.

I dialed 911 and saw the agents running towards the scene. I asked for the ambulance and, suddenly, there were people, lights, and action. I moved closer as I finalized my request for an ambulance to the arboretum. Margaret was talking to Brenda.

"Hang in there, Brenda. You can do it," Margaret said.

"I loved Sheila," Brenda said through the pain. She gritted her teeth. "I wasn't going to let her shoot you, Margaret."

"Don't talk," Margaret said. "You're going to make it, just be strong."

The ambulance was coming, and Marx picked up my gun and empty casing and put his unused gun in his coat pocket. I wouldn't know why he did that for a long time, but it would make sense. After everyone was gone, on our way back down the path, he took his gun and threw it in the pond. We walked out of the arboretum together and wondered how it was that I came to know this guy, Andy Marx. We had been through a lot together and in some strange way, two guys with absolutely nothing in common, became friends.

The two ambulances sped away, one carrying a dead Allison Branch and one carrying Brenda Jackson. Brenda might make it, and we would check on her later. Margaret was taken by the police for questioning. Marx and I were going to be there for her.

We got to the parking lot and Marx got in his car. There would be a lot to do to close this case. He rubbed his eyes that looked worn and scarred from all that he had seen and all that he had to do as a detective. He knew, and I knew, that it was time and that soon he would be gone from this work that had aged him way beyond his years. He had done his job well and with integrity. He had very little to regret, except for the fact he had to kill in the line of duty. It always haunted him the times he had to do that. It would also haunt me for years to come. That I DID fire that shot, that I did help end a life, something I thought I could never have done. But it was over. SHE was gone from my life for good. Maybe not from my dreams, which I am sure will come. But from my life, the danger of HER haunting me daily was gone. The only thing keeping me from my redemption was... well, me.

CHAPTER 42

I called Katy from the parking lot. Of course, she had already seen the news. She had been waiting nervously throughout the whole ordeal. She had contact with me only from what she saw on the news.

"Can you come by?" she asked. "I just have to talk to you. I was so scared that something bad may happen to you."

"Sure, I can. I'm okay, but I need talk to you, too. I can't believe that this is over and that SHE no longer has that hold over all of us." It's been a few years and now, I finally feel I can get my life back. We all can get our lives back. You, me, Marx, and Margaret, too."

"Mike, is she truly dead?" she asked. "I mean, I hate to say it that way, but she was so evil," Katy said.

"I think many of us are better off now that she is gone. I think, finally, we can put this story to bed and get back to a normal life." *Yeah, right, like you believe your life will return to normal.*

"Look, Katy, I'll come by when I get back to town.

Marx and I have a few more things to take care of. As soon as that is done, I'll call, and we will get together. I missed you, and I was scared I wasn't coming back. I'll see you soon." I hung up and then got back into the car with Marx. We were on our way home. And, the word home sounded good.

We said little the first fifteen minutes of the ride. Both of us seemed lost in our own thoughts. Mine were about this final episode and how it had played out. I had shot someone. It was something I didn't think I could do. I assumed Marx was thinking back on his career and how it was just about over. But Marx had kept me out of legal trouble, and, in fact, Andy Marx had saved my life more than once. This time was no different. Then he would walk off into the sunset and retire. Just like that. A career he loved and enjoyed for so many years would be over. I looked over and studied his face. I could tell he was struggling with coming to grips with the end. It's something we all do in this life when we know something is over. It's called acceptance and when something is over for us, something that changes us, we are supposed to accept and move on. Actually, it is much harder than that. Some people never do accept and get lost in every moment of the past without looking ahead to the future. I could see Marx was looking ahead and behind. It was like a teenager who wants to be a grown up and be independent yet looks back to his parents for the security they need. Andy Marx's security was his job for so many years and now he would be venturing out into something new, something he was not accustomed to. I had to ask.

"Hey, Marx, I know you're deep in thought, and, you don't have to say, if you don't want to, but are you thinking about the end, I mean, the end of being a detective?" I asked.

"Well, yes, just a little," he replied. "But more I am thinking of Branch and how that woman got so messed up. In some ways, I felt sorry for her."

"I guess I did, too. But I had to ask myself, why? how?"

"Here's what I feel and maybe you feel the same way. I competed and wanted to be first. First in my class, first on the force, lead detective, all of that. But I never considered what was wrong with her. I just thought she was just a little over-the-top jealous and had a hard time being number two. I didn't see deep enough that she was hurt in some way, some way I could not fathom. I just didn't do enough. I had to be willing to shoot her because she was sowing evil everywhere she went. I had to keep her from killing other people. I just wish I had gotten her to a good shrink. She was a pretty good cop in the beginning. I just misread her for so long. Maybe I could have helped."

"Look, you did everything you could. We both did, but for me and you, for both of us, we may never forget what happened. I think this will forever be etched in our memories and in our souls. You're a good man, Andy. But we both may remember this for more what we missed than what we did see. For that, I see that we both have gained a bit of redemption, knowing that we still didn't feel good about her being gone, even though it had to happen. Like she used to say, 'it was destiny'.

"Yeah, it could be that way. You and I have a lot to think about, Mike. Our lives are so similar, yet, different. But we both need a change and whether that is good or bad remains to be seen. I guess it's what we make of the change, and, actually, why we are making the change," Marx said.

"Words that could drive me to the right place,

Marx." *Redemption is a reclaiming process. One in which you weigh so many options and the danger of choosing the wrong one puts you several lengths back in the race. You do change. Everyone does. Even when you don't want them to, events change you.*

"It's just what I think. It doesn't make it all true," he said, studying the road before him.

"But, you're smart enough for me to take those words to heart." *Why we are making the change? Why?*

We were silent the rest of the way home. Somehow, I felt like it might be the last time we talked. I mean talking about real life things. I had no idea if we would stay friends or not, but I wanted to. Andy Marx helped make a change in me. So did some others, people I was lucky to encounter these last few years of my life, especially, my favorite bartender, Katy.

▲

I called Katy as soon as Marx had dropped me off at my place and I got my things put away. It was good to be home and back to a familiar place. I had been in many places, all in the chase of someone I once fell in love with for a short time. I had no idea she wanted to kill me. From Sheila's suicide to now, I had escaped danger, lived through some nightmares, and fell in and out of love. Katy answered her phone.

"Hello, Mike."

"Hello, Katy."

"It's so good to hear your voice," she said. "I have really missed you and was so worried about you."

"There's so much to tell you. The story was just too crazy to believe. But now, that it's almost over, I need to tell it to you and vent a little. I was hoping I could come over in a bit?" I asked.

"Of course," she replied. "But please make it sooner than later! I really need to see you."

"I need to be with you, too. I'll be there shortly," I said and hung up.

I got my keys and headed out of the door. The drive was short, or so it seemed. I made it there in fifteen minutes and that was record time. I got out of the car, locked it and made my way up sidewalk to Katy's place. I rang the bell and she quickly came to the door to let me in. I got inside the door and she threw her arms around me and kissed me. I felt a passion, something I hadn't felt for quite some time. I was not confused about how Katy felt about me, nor was I really confused about how I felt about Katy.

"I missed you so much. I was so worried," she said looking into my eyes. She laid her head on my chest, her arms around me squeezing.

This girl really made feel special, and she loved me unconditionally. I wanted to love her the same way. We went to the living room and sat. I told her all that happened from the time we went to Florida and then all the way back to Downers Grove. She listened intently and asked some questions, but after the story was told she had a few more to ask.

"Did you ever think of saving her?" Or, did you know it would always be a showdown?" she asked.

"Well, I think I always knew it would be a showdown but, at the same time, I felt for her. She was so damaged, and her face was so disfigured. I couldn't hardly look at her. But her mind was so damaged, too, that I felt bad for her. She was in another world when we got to the arboretum," I said looking out the window.

Katy seemed to catch me thinking here and was wondering what I really felt for Branch to begin with, but she was kind enough not to ask at this point. The story of Allison was told and I held her hands in mine, looking into her gorgeous eyes. At this very moment, it was all that I needed. Then she asked one more question.

"I just have to know, Mike. Did you shoot her, did you pull the trigger?" she asked.

I stumbled with this question for a few seconds. *Truth, not half-truth, the full truth.* "I did fire and hit her, but Marx threw his gun away in the pond and kept my gun and casings. No one can know this except you, Marx, and me. If that got out there will be more difficult questions to answer, and it may even get Marx in trouble. Between you and me, yes, but for everyone else in the world, the answer is no."

Katy sat and pondered the answer and then moved closer to me. She kissed me once more and for a short time, the rest of the morning, she made me forget the story. *Why do I make the change? It's the reason I change, right?* We slept for several hours and we both needed it.

My dream was one I had had before but a bit different. The two little men both standing on my shoulders. One on the left was telling me all the things that I was wrong about and the one on the right telling me I had chosen a better way, that I was going to be better. This time the story was no longer about Allison Branch, kidnapping, murder, explosions or shootings. This time it was about Katy.

"So many times, you overlooked Katy. But really, she was always there, even when you didn't know it," the man on the right said.

The man on the left broke in, *"There will be so many others, why pick just one, Mikey?"*

"She loves you unconditionally, Mike. No matter if you treated her badly or put her aside, she was there for you, always," the man on the right said.

"You don't love her back unconditionally, do you? You'll let her down and you won't always be there for her, will you?"

"But you do love her."

"You'll just hurt her, too, just like the others," the guy on the left said.

"No, he won't, he loves her!" the man on the right said loudly. *"She's **the reason** he changed."*

"He knows nothing about reasons, he just does because I tell him to."

I jumped straight up awake and startled Katy from her sleep.

"Are you okay?" she asked.

"I'm fine, just a dream... a bad one but I'm sure I'll shake it off." I said still watching the two men argue in my mind.

I'm not better, but I will get better. I must. But remember, must fight because for you, Mike, nothing has been easy, either by your own choices or by what life delivered to your doorstep. Some of it you deserved and some you did not. Redemption is something worth fighting for and whether you deserved life's outcomes or not, there is still one thing more important than anything else, and that is to love unconditionally. You must try. You have to fight. It's worth it to your soul.

EPILOGUE

Six months later...

I don't really know why I went to the cemetery when Allison Branch was buried. Marx had filled me in on when and where and we both went. *There was no one else there. Her only friend left on the planet, Brenda Jackson, was in jail. There was no service, no eulogy, no remembrances, and no one else was there. It was a sad scene, really. Just Marx and I standing there in the cool spring breeze, making sure there was someone there to lay the body to rest in a grave next to her mother.*

I think back on that day six months before and wonder why we did that and wonder why I even still think about it today while fishing with my brother, James. It was early October and the breeze on the lake was sharp. It was beginning to cool off in Wisconsin.

As the boat drifted along the windy and choppy

lake, I began to finally feel that maybe this story of murder, prison sentences, trials, and tests of wills were just stories that were meant to teach me something. Maybe it was just a book I read or a dream in the night, and, that it really didn't happen at all. But, in fact, it had happened, and the story was real. I finally had over the last six months, recognized what had happened to each of us. There was sort of a redemption for each of us. I found out that many good things had happened to many of us over the last six months, but there were scars that would last a long time. A lifetime in fact.

What redemption was for each character was hard to pin down. But over time, I think I was able to decide, in my own mind, what their redemption was.

For Margaret, she had been through the difficult deaths of her daughter and her husband. She had tried hard to avenge those deaths and was there at the end. Thankfully, she didn't kill anyone. Margaret was just too sweet of a lady for that to be hanging over her head the rest of her time on this earth. Through that last event she found a new strength to overcome all that had happened to her. Knowing she tried to avenge Sheila's death was all that she had needed to feel like she had not let it go but had tried to make it right for Sheila. I respected Margaret for that, and we would remain friends for a long time.

As for Brenda, her redemption was stepping in front of that bullet that was meant for Margaret. Brenda never wanted to be involved in all of this, but, through her late sister, Breanne, she had been pulled into this saga. Margaret visited her in prison and in some way, visiting Brenda allowed her to keep some connection to Sheila. Brenda's time in prison would be long, but she would always look forward to Margaret's visits.

For Katy, she had endured two kidnappings and many disappointments at the hands of yours truly. Her redemption came in the form of her recognizing her own strength as a woman, one who could be independent and not depend on someone else for her happiness. This was not an easy process for Katy. She had struggled and argued with herself for years, telling herself in the end that she just wasn't good enough. But these times and experiences had changed Katy. Yes, she still loved me, and I don't think that is ever going to change. Katy is smart enough to know not to try and change me, but instead to try re-mold me.

For Marx, he now had a new job as a private detective. He had retired from the force two weeks after the ordeal at Downers Grove. Deep down, he never tried to beat Allison Branch. His competitiveness kept him sharp, but he really didn't want her to lose. He knew her story after being her partner for so long and the fact that she turned into a bad cop was the reason he needed to bring her to justice. It was always the ethics with Andy. He always seemed to do what was right. His redemption was to escape HER. He had finally put to bed all the myriad of emotions he had about this case. His life felt new again and he seemed to grow younger by the day. He would never be "smart ass partner guy" to me again. He would be my friend, someone I respected, someone I could look up to. He had his own demons to deal with, but day by day, they seemed to disappear and a happiness returned to him, a happiness that seemed to elude him throughout this deadly episode.

Carrianne had found love and it was someone that could give her all the things she had wanted. Although she had struggled with the fact, she had turned on everyone she had known in her life, including Jake, she knew in her heart what she had wanted and needed and that was to love someone and have a family of her own. We would never see her again, but we did find out from a reliable source, that she was pregnant and expecting eight months from now. I think that I was truly happy for her. She was the one of all of us that probably had the most pain to endure to reach a complete redemption in her life. I respected that. A lot.

Well, that leaves me. I still find myself to be a work in progress. I had experienced many things that I was ill-prepared to experience. Smarter people could have waded through it much better than I did. I wondered why the vengeful people I encountered wanted to inflict the maximum punishment on others that had somehow hurt them in some way. The people like Breanne, Andres, The Boss, Aberto, The Chemist, Allison Branch, and Jerry Linhart. I was not that much different than them. I found that it was okay to feel angry, hurt, or even feel that you wanted to get back at others for your pain. Yet, I felt that I was the architect of my own pain and I wanted to point the finger at others, hoping that they would suffer the same pain or more than me. That is what is wrong with the worst in all of us. It created the feeling that I may never be accountable to myself or to others. It was a lesson that I learned the hard way. Life was too short to harbor these kinds of feelings for others that went over the top.

So, am I feeling more accountable every day for me? I could say yes, but how ironic that liquor could be my worst enemy at times, yet my favorite bartender may have been the one to save me? She did make me see some things in me that were not good, and she didn't just push them to the side. Yet she didn't condemn me for it, but tried to help me through it. There is a difference between condemnation and pointing out the problem and helping with the solution. Her help was easy to accept. It was her kindness and patience that helped me to see. Sometimes I think God puts people in your life to make a difference. That is, if you have the patience to listen and have an open heart. The difference, between me now and back then, is that I am not such a closed-hearted person and I have more patience to be still and listen than I used to have. I can see me better and be accountable for my own life.

The little man on my left shoulder could always let me blame someone else. The little man on my right was becoming more dominant now. I'm not saying that I'm without sin. Not at all, quite the contrary. But at least now, I think I can find my way through a world full of temptation and traps that lay all around. To be at peace more with myself.

"Hey, Mike, you got one!" James yelled as my fishing pole had bent over full.

It took a couple of minutes to get that one in and it was a nice walleye. I smiled at James and said, "Hey, you got one too, brother!" His pole bending over like mine did.

"Doubles," he said as he used the term we had used when we caught a fish at the same time.

It really didn't get much better than that.

We ended the day back at the cabin and fried up the walleye we caught. James had gone home shortly after we cleaned up. I sat with a scotch on the porch looking out on the lake. I rocked in the rocker on the screened in porch. I heard the knock on the door and got up to answer it and I unlocked the door and slowly opened it.

"Well, hello there, handsome."

"Well, hello, Dear Katy. If it's not my favorite bartender," I said smiling.

As I put my arms around Katy and she lay her head against my chest, I began to realize that as unlucky as I once had been, my new life was feeling complete. We stood together in silence for a while, looking out at the sun shining a long beam across the lake, making silver sparkles on the water. We were both safe now, and, somehow, all that I thought I would never have, I now had with Katy. We both had come full circle to a place where we could both feel it in our souls. The one word that seemed to avoid us, go around us, and pass us by, had finally come home to reside with us both.

Redemption had come home to stay.

Made in the USA
Monee, IL
08 January 2022

88473978R00148